HAR

Take a look at our books for September!

A marriage ended or a marriage mended? Kayla has been bought back by her estranged husband, billionaire Duardo Alvarez, in Helen Bianchin's scorcher *Purchased by the Billionaire*. Bedded for revenge or wedded for passion? Freya has made the mistake of hiding the existence of Italian Enrico Ranieri's little son, and she must make amends as his convenient wife in Michelle Reid's torrid tale *The Ranieri Bride*. Is revenge sweet? Greek tycoon Christos Carides certainly thinks so when he seduces Becca Summer in Kim Lawrence's sizzling story, *The Carides Pregnancy*. But for how long? Out for the count? Italian aristocrat Alessio Ramontella certainly thinks he's KO'd innocent English beauty Laura, but will she actually succumb to his ruthless seduction? Find out in *The Count's Blackmail Bargain* by Sara Craven. Meantime, Carol Marinelli's mixing business with intense pleasure in her new UNCUT novel, *Taken for His Pleasure*. It's a gold band of blackmail for temporary bride Maddison as she's forced to marry wealthy Greek Demetrius Papasakis in *The Greek's Convenient Wife* by Melanie Milburne. Mistress material? Nora Lang doesn't think she's got what it takes in Susan Napier's *Mistress for a Weekend*. But tycoon Blake MacLeod thinks Nora definitely has something special—confidential information. And he'll keep her in his bed to prevent her giving it away. Finally, an ultimatum...*The Marriage Ultimatum* by Helen Brooks. It's Carter Blake's only option when Liberty refuses to let him take her.

FOR *Love* OR MONEY

Romance on the red carpet!

FOR LOVE OR MONEY is the ultimate
reading experience for the reader who loves
Presents books, and who also has a taste
for tales of wealth and celebrity—
and the accompanying gossip and scandal!

Look out for the special covers.

Michelle Reid

THE RANIERI BRIDE

FOR Love OR MONEY

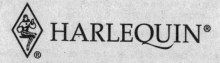

HARLEQUIN®

TORONTO • NEW YORK • LONDON
AMSTERDAM • PARIS • SYDNEY • HAMBURG
STOCKHOLM • ATHENS • TOKYO • MILAN • MADRID
PRAGUE • WARSAW • BUDAPEST • AUCKLAND

ISBN-13: 978-0-373-12564-7
ISBN-10:   0-373-12564-X

THE RANIERI BRIDE

First North American Publication 2006.

This edition published by arrangement with Harlequin Books S.A.

® and TM are trademarks of the publisher. Trademarks indicated with
® are registered in the United States Patent and Trademark Office, the
Canadian Trade Marks Office and in other countries.

www.eHarlequin.com

Printed in U.S.A.

All about the author…
Michelle Reid

Reading has been an important part of
MICHELLE REID's life as far back as she can
remember. She was encouraged by her mother,
who made the twice-weekly bus trip to the
nearest library, to keep feeding this particular
hunger. In fact, one of Michelle's most abiding
memories from those days is coming home from
school to find a newly borrowed selection of
books stacked on the kitchen table just waiting to
be delved into.

There has not been a day since that she hasn't
had at least two books lying open somewhere
in the house ready to pick up and continue
whenever she has a quiet moment.

Her love of romance fiction has always been
strong, though she feels she was quite late in
discovering the riches Harlequin has to offer.
It wasn't long after making this discovery that
she made the daring decision to try her hand
at writing a Presents book for herself, never
expecting it to become such an important part
of her life.

Now she shares her time between her large,
close, lively family and writing. She lives with her
husband in a tiny white-stoned cottage in the
English Lake district. It is both a romantic haven
and the perfect base to go walking through some
of the most beautiful scenery in England.

CHAPTER ONE

ENRICO RANIERI was striding across Hannard's foyer with his dark head lowered. He was late and he was frowning, too preoccupied with the meeting he was about to attend to notice the drop-jaw looks of recognition he and his small entourage were receiving as they passed through.

It was the finest—*finest*—hint of a sound crashing into his consciousness that made him lift up his head. After that he stopped dead, every important thought preceding this moment wiped clean away by the sight that met his ink-dark gaze.

She was about ten feet away, just stepping out of one of the lifts. His insides flipped and then rolled as if he'd been put into a sudden steep dive. He struggled to believe it—or did not want to. It was years since he'd so much as clapped eyes on her, yet as she uttered some small, indistinguishable sound he found himself rendered so immobile he couldn't make his brain move beyond the fact that she was right there before him in the flesh!

She had not noticed him yet because her head was

lowered, her glorious mane of bright auburn hair caught up on the top of her head in one of those unflattering knots that had always challenged him to tug it free.

It challenged him again now, setting a couple of nerves flicking in his fingers, while something far more potent flicked at other parts of him.

Freya…

Her name sizzled across his senses in a tight, complicated mix of hate and pleasure. Three years ago he'd kicked her out of his life without conscience, then spent the next memorable year taking that decision out on anyone who fancied taking him on. Business or pleasure, he had not been fussy. She had worked for him. He'd trusted her. No woman before or since had ever earned that level of trust. She'd lived in his apartment and slept in his bed. He slept alone now and any physical activities always took place somewhere else.

In fact, she'd stolen so much away from him, it was no wonder he was sizzling with hate.

But—*Dio*—she looked good. Even wearing that unflattering grey suit, which looked at least one size too big for her, she was stinging his senses with first-hand knowledge of what lay hidden beneath the layers of high-street-cheap.

Like the clothes she used to wear before he'd taken her in hand and turned the scrappy sow's ear into a breathtakingly beautiful silk purse.

That odd feeling moved to his chest, turning into a swirling, coiling stab of discomfort when he remembered how she had left all the silk behind when he'd kicked her out.

Now here she was, walking towards him with her

head tilted downwards as if she was as preoccupied with her thoughts as he had been with his. His eyes narrowed as he watched her come closer. A fine layer of sweat went bristling across the surface of his skin as he waited for the silken arc of her gold-tipped eyelashes to lift up and show him a pair of vivid green eyes destined to turn as dark as his own with shock.

He wanted to see her shock—needed to see it, like a man possessed with a fevered desire to watch another human being squirm.

Did she work at Hannard's? Had he unwittingly logged into a way to make the beautiful but deceiving Freya Jenson pay yet again for what she had done to him?

His white teeth came together with a snap of tension as he waited for the glinting red head to lift up. She was almost upon him. Hell, his senses were going crazy. Any second now she was going to cannon right into him! Anticipation leapt inside him like a mad, snarling wolf ready to attack.

She pulled to a stop suddenly and all of that swirling, tingling war of feeling completely blanketed him because he thought she had sensed his presence at last.

Then he heard her speak—

'No, Nicky,' she said. 'It's no use trying to pull free of my hand when you *know* Mummy is not going to let it go.'

Like a man hurled from a storm into a maelstrom, Enrico dropped his gaze downward. If his senses had made a violent dive when he'd first seen her, it was nothing to what he experienced now as his eyes came to rest on the small denim-clad boy who was fighting to get free of her restraining hand.

Curling black hair crowned a handsome little face,

and a pair of fiercely determined ink-black eyes glared up at his mother.

Nicky, he thought.

Nicolo, he extended.

She had named her son Nicolo.

Right there in Hannard's foyer, Enrico Ranieri, hard-headed businessman and cold, ruthless operator, quite simply crashed and burned.

The 'terrible twos' were an apt label when it came to her son, Freya thought ruefully as she fought to keep a grip on his hand. Give him the chance and he'd be off causing mayhem wherever he could wreak it. Lose concentration on him for a single second and he became a terrifying danger to himself.

She was going to have to purchase leading reins, she decided as she stood waging battle with one determined little boy. They would cause serious offence to his dignity, but hanging on to a writhing, kicking two-year-old meant that she was in danger of hurting him in her effort to keep him contained.

'The park,' she said, using a favoured destination as a key to unlock the door to her son's more compliant side. 'Be a good boy and walk nicely, and we will go to the park.'

'Monkeys,' he replied.

'No,' Freya returned firmly. 'The monkeys live at the zoo. The park is closer.'

'I like monkeys.'

'I have hold of one right here,' she laughed. 'Be a good boy today, and we will go and see the monkeys tomorrow when we have more—'

'He's mine,' a deep voice rasped like coarse sandpaper across her exposed nape.

Freya actually shivered, the blood in her veins beginning to freeze before she'd even lifted up her head and let her eyes clash with a pair of black eyes that flashed with raw hostility.

Her heart gave a shocked thump against her ribcage, then almost stopped altogether. It was like being hit over the head by your worst nightmare, she likened as she stared at six feet three inches of hard masculine aggression standing right over her and threatening hell. The black hair, the black eyes, the almost-black suit covering his tightly muscled framework, even the shiny black shoes on his long, narrow feet, all screamed: *The devil has come to collect.*

'No,' she breathed, not wanting to believe that Enrico, of all the rotten people in the world she could possibly meet again, was standing less than two feet away.

'*Madre de Dio,* he *is!*' Enrico bit out on a hushed, driven hiss of sizzling fury.

Freya blinked, still too locked in shock to realise that he had misunderstood her choked little negative. Then she watched his eyes drop to her son and fire up with the most ungodly flame of possessive rage.

Even Nicky was affected by that fierce look. Instead of continuing to tug on Freya's hand, he clung tightly to it and shifted his wiry little body behind her legs. It was that defensive move from her normally fearless little boy that made anger burn out the deep freeze of her shock. With a lifting of her chin, Freya looked the hard, cruel, unrelenting devil right in the eye and repeated coldly, 'No, he is not.'

Enrico moved with a tight shift of his lean body. 'Don't lie to me,' he rasped out, dragging his eyes away from the little boy to fix back on his mother's face. 'You ruthless witch. I am going to make you pay for this!'

Freya could see that he meant it by the murderous glint in his eyes and that thin-lipped way in which he was holding his mouth. An attractive mouth once, she found herself thinking, a gorgeously knowing and very seductive mouth. Like the rest of him: gorgeously sexy and disgustingly aware of it.

'I don't know what you're talking about,' she denied stiffly.

Black eyes flared. He took a step towards her. For a horrible moment, Freya thought he was going to take hold of her by the throat. She gasped and took a step backwards, almost tripping over her son.

'Enrico...' Someone placed a warning hand on his arm.

It was only then that Freya became aware again of where it was they were standing. The whole foyer had gone silent and dozens of curious faces were turned on them. Enrico appeared to have forgotten his own entourage, one member of which was trying to remind him that they had an audience.

He glanced around, soot-black eyelashes flickering against fiercely jutting cheekbones. The whole structure of his lean, attractive face was savagely clenched. The atmosphere in the foyer was fizzing and popping with his barely contained violence, which he swung away from Freya and turned onto the person touching his arm.

Freya shuddered. Her grip on her son must have loosened in that mad moment of relief, because Nicky suddenly broke away from her. In the split second it took her to swing round to try and recapture the small boy he was already out of reach and heading straight for the exit like a mini-hostage suddenly set free.

Nicky knew those exit doors and exactly how to make them work: break the magic beam and they would swing open on a whole world of excitement for a small and fearless two-year-old.

'Nicky—no!' Freya cried out and went running after him.

He just gave a squeal of delight and kept going, little legs carrying him ever closer to freedom and the narrow pavement outside, which was the only point of safety between him and one of London's busiest streets. Freya was already seeing his little body crushed beneath the wheels of a double-decker bus as she ran. Her skin had gone clammy, her heart was pounding agonisingly in her breast.

Then an arm reached out and a big body bent to scoop the child right off the ground. As Freya watched it happen through a haze of wild terror, she found her eyes fixing on yet another sickeningly familiar face.

Fredo Scarsozi, Enrico's long-term bodyguard, was holding her son in a circle of formidable muscle-bound power. Her stomach rolled over. Nicky was yelling in frustrated temper while Fredo stood looking down at him—just looking.

Fredo could see the resemblance too, she realised as she skidded to a halt in front of him.

'Give him to me,' she demanded breathlessly, holding out her arms for her son.

Fredo switched his gaze to her face and did nothing. True, unfettered fear closed her throat off and congealed her blood. Nicky suddenly stopped yelling, the curiosity value of being held by this big man winning over his protests, and an inquisitive frown puckered his face.

'Please,' Freya begged, lifting her arms higher.

The husky wobble in her voice grabbed her son's attention. She was trembling all over. A restless stir was starting up around the foyer because the onlookers were uncomfortable with what was happening here, though they were not sure as to what that actually was.

Then Fredo switched his gaze to a place over her right shoulder. Icy fingers of dread stroked right down Freya's spine because she knew he was looking to Enrico for instructions. One negative glint from those angry black eyes and it would take an army to drag her son free.

'Monkey?' Nicky questioned, and startled the tough Fredo Scarsozi into glancing at him. Then the big man's mouth stretched into a reluctant grin.

'*Gratzi, bambino,*' he murmured drily.

Nicky grinned, too, all white baby teeth and excruciating little-boy charm.

'Please give him back to me,' Freya begged unsteadily.

'Do as she says,' Enrico coldly put in.

Heart thundering out of control now, Freya didn't look round, didn't breathe, didn't do anything but stand there and wait for her son to arrive safely back where he belonged. As Fredo handed him over, her arms closed around that precious little body so tightly that Nicky let out a protest, but she didn't—couldn't—slacken her grip.

One final wild glance into Fredo's knowing face and then she and Nicky were out of the Hannard building as if the wild dogs of hell were after them.

Which was not far from what Enrico was about to put on their tails.

'Go after her,' he instructed Fredo.

With a nod, the bodyguard moved off with a muscle-bound lope that belied his lightness of foot.

Enrico turned and looked at the frozen crowd in the foyer. His expression was controlled now, the trampling mayhem that had been going on inside him grimly crushed to a low burn. His small clutch of assistants just stood there staring at him as if he'd lost his sanity. Others—complete strangers to him—were staring at him with fascination that was tinged with recognition and also understanding as to what his presence here had to mean.

Trouble—*big* trouble.

Enrico Ranieri was known throughout Europe as an acquirer of struggling businesses, a troubleshooter notorious for taking no prisoners as he worked to turn ailing companies' fortunes around.

And he always struck without warning—a tactic that gave him the quick upper hand. So when Enrico turned up in your foyer, you didn't only stop and stare, you felt your own vulnerability right through to your shoes.

When he was confronting one of your own, because she happened to have her child with her, you could see his reputation for ruthless throat-cutting acted out before your horrified eyes.

They think I dislike children, Enrico realised. They think they are seeing Hannard's crèche being wiped out with a swift, decisive flick of my hand. And maybe I will do it, he thought brutally, as his cold eyes dismissed every one of them and he strode across the foyer and into one of the lifts.

He stabbed a button then turned to watch his now wary entourage rush to get into the carriage before the doors closed. No one spoke. They had the sense not to. He felt as if he'd been turned to a pillar of stone. Nothing was going on inside him now—nothing other than—

Freya had given birth to his son.

The lift stopped and the doors slid open at the executive top floor, where he was met by yet another sea of faces forming an anxious wall of greeting in front of him.

Enrico did not want it. He did not want anything to do with damned business right now. He wanted...

As he stepped out of the lift, the icy shards glinting in his eyes had the wall of suits parting in front of him, welcoming smiles withering, the hands half lifted to shake his hand dropping nervously away.

'This way, Mr Ranieri,' some brave soul prompted.

He nodded, flat lipped, and followed while everyone else fell into silent step behind. He was shown into a large office filled with light spilling in from wall-to-wall windows. Enrico stood for a couple of seconds taking in nothing—nothing, until the silent tension behind him finally got to him and he turned.

Ignoring each wary face but for that of Carlo, his PA, he instructed, 'I want the personal profiles of every employee sent to my laptop within the next ten minutes.'

The Hannard suits shifted on a tidal wave of discomfort. His personal staff were wise enough to keep their body language under control.

'Postpone the board meeting until tomorrow. And I will want to meet anyone with decision-making powers before it begins.' He continued his instruction like a shark circling its next meal. 'That is all.'

It was a dismissal. He turned his back on the lot of them before he strode over to the carefully cleared and freshly polished desk that used to belong to Josh Hannard but now was his. Behind him the shuffle of a mass exit began to take place.

'But we thought we were going to have a working lunch so we could introduce everybody,' he heard someone mutter in hushed bewilderment.

'If I were you, I would skip lunch and start boning up on what it is you do here to earn your salary,' one of his own people advised.

'But Mr Hannard—'

'Mr Hannard is no longer in charge here, Mr Ranieri is. And he has a nasty habit of chewing on spare flesh and spitting out the bones.'

Enrico smiled as he heard that. Quite a character reference, he mused thinly. Then he lifted his eyes to the rooftop view of London he could see through the window and the smile died.

His son—*his son*!

'*Cagna,*' he muttered. *She* was going to pay for this! He, Enrico Ranieri, was going to chew on Freya Jenson's delectable flesh and spit out her deceiving, lying, cheating bones!

* * *

Freya sat on the grass in the park surrounded by ducks while her son fed them the remains of her uneaten sandwiches—and she shivered despite the heat of the summer sun.

Icy cold was how she always felt when she let herself think about Enrico. Hurt, hatred and contempt could turn a warm-blooded woman to a block of ice.

So could fear.

Of the unknown.

Of what Enrico was going to do next.

She shifted, blinking her green eyes as a hungry beak pecked at her fingers. Relinquishing the small crust to the greedy duck, she turned to Nicky, who was sitting there in his element, smiling—and looking so much more like his father than she'd ever let herself see before, that it came as a shock each time she gazed at him now.

Now that she had seen his father in the flesh again.

Now that she had seen the grown-up version of her son's handsome face, those black eyes, the stubborn mouth and determined chin.

The fact that Enrico had been so quick to recognise himself in Nicky had shaken her to her very roots. How dared he—how *dared* he do that after all he'd said and done to disown responsibility?

She'd come to hate him for doing that.

'Get out of my life,' he'd ripped at her three years ago. 'You are a cheat and a slut and I never want to see you again so long as I live.'

Bitter, cold, heartless. Arrogant, superior, judgemental; deaf…

She ran out of adjectives and made do with a sigh instead.

Maybe he'd had second thoughts about Nicky by now, she thought hopefully. He might have seen a miniature mirror image of himself in her little boy, but there again his cousin Luca was yet another reflection of those disgustingly handsome Ranieri features. A sly, mean, nasty mirror of Enrico, but the likeness was there, and Enrico would have remembered that by now and dismissed her and Nicky out of his nasty suspicious—

Then it hit her—the one thing she had been trying very hard *not* to think about.

What had he been doing in Hannard's foyer, anyway?

He hadn't bought Hannard's—had he? He wasn't about to become her boss again?

Her spine tensed up as nerve ends crashed together, her cold fingers twisting tightly on her lap. No, she thought— no! Don't look for the worst-case scenario. He could have just been passing through. Maybe he was a friend of Josh Hannard and was only meeting him for lunch.

And maybe pigs can fly, she was then forced to tell herself. When Enrico Ranieri appeared in a company's foyer with his faithful entourage stacking up behind him, then he was there for only one purpose.

It was a buy-out and, with his usual tactics, he was making a surprise hit on a new acquisition like a lethal bolt of lightning striking out of the blue.

A shiver ran down her back. Oh, no, she thought, and lowered her face to her knees because she just couldn't face the idea of him having the power to ruin her life—again.

Once had been enough.

Once upon a time three years ago she'd had a wonderful job as his personal assistant. She'd lived a wonderful life as his live-in lover. They'd barely survived being out of each other's sight. Two hot lovers with passionate and feverishly possessive temperaments, they'd matched each other, fire for sizzling fire.

Then she'd met his cousin and within weeks it was all over.

'Monkey,' Nicky said levelly.

'We will see the monkeys tomorrow,' Freya promised, lifting her head to look at this dark-haired little boy who was the most important thing in her life—whoever his father was.

'No, monkey over there,' he insisted, pointing with a finger.

Turning her head, Freya found her eyes fixing on the bulky shape of Fredo Scarsozi. He was standing beneath the shade of a tree not twenty feet from them. As she stared he sent her a brief nod in acknowledgement and she knew then, knew with every single fractured nerve she possessed that, far from dismissing them, Enrico was right there watching them from behind the steady gaze of his most trusted employee.

Well, this was one fight he was going to have with himself because she was not going to play any part in it, she decided as she clambered to her feet. Nicky was her son and only hers, and it was going to be up to Enrico to prove otherwise.

If he cared enough.

Bitterness welled, and anger—a hard, cold rod of contempt that straightened her spine as she held a hand out to her son.

'Come on, sweetie,' she murmured. 'It's time for us to go back now.'

Nicky came without argument. With no bread left, the ducks had scooted back into the pond. Plus her son was used to the routine he had been living with since he was three months old and she had been so very fortunate to land a job at Hannard's with its crèche all ready and waiting to take in her son.

The job itself might be basic and the pay reflected the money it cost her to place Nicky in day care, but at least he was right there in the same building with her and she could see him whenever she needed to. Their little flat might be poky and erring towards shabby but they managed.

They were happy—content to have just each other. They did not need a man in their lives and once Enrico had recovered from the shock of seeing them he would realise that he could not want anything to do with them.

'The monkey is following us,' Nicky informed her.

'He's not a monkey, he's a man,' Freya corrected and refused to glance back at Fredo—*refused*.

But that cold chill was striking at her again, the grim knowledge that she was lying to herself if she dared to believe that Enrico was going to let her off the hook without knowing the truth.

He was ruthless and tenacious.

CHAPTER TWO

LYING, cheating, vindictive whore…

Enrico sat behind the desk, silently throwing those insults at the photograph sourced from Hannard's security files that looked out at him from his computer screen.

She looked so cute, so sweetly innocent, he mocked acidly. As if butter would not melt in her mouth.

But it did melt.

With a flick of the mouse he blanked her out by pulling up a photograph of the boy and once again felt that soul-shattering, crash-and-burn feeling rock his insides.

'What do you think—is he mine or Luca's?' he asked Fredo.

Fredo gave one of his shrugs. 'If he is Luca's, then the *bambino* has been fortunate enough to miss out on his papa's less savoury genes,' the bodyguard said drily before adding quietly, 'He has your eyes and mouth and your—stubbornness. He also has your sense of fun…'

Fredo was thinking about the way the boy had kept glancing up to check on him all the way back here and the cheeky smile he'd worn on his little mouth. As they'd entered the building he'd turned and shouted,

'Bye, monkey!' before being dragged off chuckling by his mamma who'd refused to glance Fredo's way at all.

Enrico did not feel as if he had so much as a drop of fun in him right now as he sat there staring at the child's face; it was as if those ink-dark eyes were making a link with his own—he could feel it right down to the dregs of his swirling, tensing gut.

'He is mine, I feel it,' he uttered gruffly.

'*Si.*' Fredo nodded.

Why the sombre confirmation from his bodyguard further creased him up Enrico did not know—but it did.

'Get down to the crèche and keep your eye on him,' he instructed.

For the first time in all the years they'd been together Fredo balked at a command. 'You want me to spend the afternoon in a nursery—with *bambinos*?'

He was horrified. Enrico looked at him. 'Who the hell else can I trust to keep an eye on him while I work this mess out?'

'But he cannot go anywhere without his mamma! She—'

Enrico got up, all lithe muscle and brooding unease. 'She could run,' he muttered. 'I cannot afford to let her disappear until I know the truth.'

Fredo was silent. He might not like the job he was being handed but he saw the possibility in what Enrico said. With a fatalistic shrug of his big shoulders he turned to the door.

'Where is Luca hiding out these days?' Enrico sent grimly after him.

Fredo paused. 'Last I heard he was in Hawaii with his latest rich *puta*.'

'Arrange to keep him there,' Enrico ordered. 'Use threats or money or both if you have to.' Though it closed up his throat to give his cousin a single euro. 'I don't need him turning up and queering this for me when he hears I have a son by Freya.'

'How will he hear it?' Fredo asked in bewilderment. Luca had been cast out of the Ranieri family; he did not even have contact with his own mother any more!

'He will hear it like the rest of the world will hear it,' Enrico said. 'When I announce it publicly that I have a son and intend to marry the boy's mother.'

There was a very thick pause, then Fredo said carefully, 'You are going too fast with this, Enrico—'

A pair of black-ice eyes lanced Fredo with a look that made the other man sigh.

'You need positive proof before you—'

'The boy is mine. I want him. The mother comes with the package.'

'Try telling the *signorina* that,' Fredo said drily.

'I intend to.'

Freya was wistfully wishing she lived on the other side of the world right now.

But she didn't. She was standing right here in Hannard's basement, mindlessly feeding paper into an old flatbed scanner so the information on it could be transferred to the mainframe computer.

Trapped, she thought bleakly, by the need to earn a living.

And frightened, because she didn't know what Enrico was going to do.

It was all over the building that he'd bought out Josh

Hannard. It was also all over the building that he'd accosted her in the foyer this lunchtime and caused an ugly scene.

Her telephone rang. It hadn't stopped ringing since she'd got back from lunch, flooding her with calls from her fellow workmates wanting her to dish the dirt as to what Mr Ranieri had said to her. The whole place was agog with curiosity and scared out of their wits for their livelihoods…more scared if they had a child in Hannard's crèche. All she could do was to lie and say, what confrontation? He was just asking about the quality of care at the crèche.

Because the real truth was way beyond her means to tell—even to herself. She didn't want to think about what it was going to mean to her and Nicky.

She picked up the phone, ready with her by now well-practised light answers.

'A Mr Scarsozi has taken up residence in the crèche,' announced the familiar voice of Cindy, its manager. 'He says he's here under instructions from our new boss to watch over Nicky. Can you tell me what the heck is going on?'

Freya closed her eyes as her heart sank to her stomach, fresh fears clenching her fingers in a tight clasp around the phone receiver. 'Has he—touched Nicky?' she asked unsteadily.

'No,' came the firm reply. 'If he tried I wouldn't let him.'

Try stopping him, Freya thought with a shiver as she recalled the way Fredo's strong arms had secured her son once already that day.

'He just stands in a corner of the playroom watching

him and scaring the rest of us half to death,' Cindy went on. 'Have you seen him, Freya? He's built like a gorilla! I want the scary thing out of my crèche!'

'Right,' Freya said, beginning to shake all over again. 'Is—is Nicky scared of him, too?'

'Are you joking? Your son had the bold cheek to go right up to him and say, "Hi, monkey, want to come and play?" Does Nicky know him?'

Now, there was a question. How did she answer it—no or yes? If she said no, she would put everyone involved in the crèche into a panic. If she said yes, she was setting herself up for more questions she had no way of answering.

'I'll deal with it,' she replied, going for the side-step response.

What did Enrico think he was doing? she wondered helplessly as she put down the phone. Was he trying to intimidate her through Nicky before he'd even—?

'Your tea break, Freya,' a frosty voice intruded. 'Though the way you've been stuck on that phone all afternoon I'd say you've already had the equivalent of several of them.'

Freya blinked, green eyes looking blankly at her head of department, a cool creature with dyed blonde hair and a tight pink mouth, who loved ruling over everyone like a tyrant.

'Be so good as to keep your personal life out of my department in future, if you don't mind.'

The woman was also miffed because, like everyone else, she'd asked Freya the same eager questions, only to receive the same stock, frustratingly unrevealing answers.

'Yes. Sorry. Right,' Freya mumbled—then she grabbed her bag and ran.

She had to talk to Enrico, and she had to do it now! Unearthing her mobile phone from her bag the moment she hit the outer corridor, she leant back against the wall and dialled into Hannard's via Reception. Her fingers were still tense, her insides shaking. She didn't want to speak to him but if she had to do it, then it was better over the phone than face-to-face.

She managed to get as far as his personal assistant—a male personal assistant—who coldly informed her that Mr Ranieri was in conference. Since Freya had once occupied the same post, she knew exactly what 'in conference' really meant. Enrico was talking to no one. He was too busy plotting her demise, no doubt.

'Look,' she said impatiently, too stressed and in need of sorting this situation out to play word games, 'I need to speak to him urgently, so you will tell him that Freya will call back in five minutes and even if he is still *in conference* I'm coming right up!'

With that she severed the connection, not wanting to hear what the PA had to say to that piece of defiance. Then she shot off to the ladies' room to use the next five minutes to freshen up.

Enrico received the message with his handsome face cut from granite. So she was panicking already. Good, he thought grimly. He wanted her to panic. He wanted her to live in fear for her life.

Freya had to wait in line for a cubicle. By the time she'd bagged one her five minutes were almost up and the panic Enrico was hoping for was really setting in. Quickly dragging her phone out of her bag, she rang into Hannard's again.

It didn't help that it took almost another two minutes to make the connection with his PA. There was a queue a mile long waiting to use the ladies', and sitting there with her panties stretched taut across her knees and a mobile telephone clamped to her ear felt pretty damn weird to say the least.

'I will put you through now, Miss Jenson,' that cold male voice informed her.

The man knew her name, which made her stomach lurch because Enrico must have told him. What else had he said? Who else had he spoken to here about her?

'I want you to leave me alone, Enrico,' she rushed out in a driven whisper the moment the connection was made. 'My son is not your son, so call off Fredo!'

'Why are you whispering?' he demanded.

'I'm *trying* to talk seriously to you without half the building hearing me!' she unleashed in an unsteady, husky hiss. 'You can't do this to me, Enrico. You can't just stroll into my life and take it over. You can't…'

Someone knocked on the cubicle door. 'You all right in there?' a female voice questioned. 'You've been in there for an age!'

'In where for an age?' Enrico rasped out.

'In the loo,' Freya answered impatiently. 'I'm in one of the loos because it happened to be where I was when my five minutes were up.'

'The loo,' he repeated, then went perfectly silent.

Freya plucked tensely at the lacy edge of her panties while she waited for him to recover from the shock. 'We all need it some time, Enrico,' she sighed out eventually. 'Even you.'

'Let me get this straight,' he gritted. 'You are speaking to me on this phone while sitting on the loo?'

'It's my afternoon break,' she explained. 'I only get ten minutes so I don't have time to…freshen up *and* talk to you unless I combine the two.'

There was another of those telling silences. Why it had to tickle at the cluster of curls between her legs, Freya didn't know—but it did.

She shifted uncomfortably. 'Enrico, call off Fredo,' she pleaded. 'He's scaring everyone!'

'Pull your pants up and get up here, Miss Jenson,' Enrico instructed coldly. 'I expect to see you standing fully dressed in my office in five minutes—and don't make me wait or you won't like what I decide to do next.'

The line went dead. Freya didn't have five minutes left of her break!

Hell, she did not have a life left if she didn't stop this craziness now, before it raced out of her control.

It was beyond her control already, her brain grimly fed to her. Muttering a few curses beneath her breath, Freya shoved her phone back into her bag and got up, then quickly rearranged her clothing while trying desperately to calm herself before she opened the cubicle door.

She was met with a sea of impatient faces…faces that lit up when they saw who she was, and her cheeks began to burn as if she'd been doing something really shocking in there. But it wasn't the length of time she'd spent locked in the loo that was making them stare at her, she admitted heavily. It was instant recognition and the curiosity value of being the woman their new boss had set upon in the foyer.

'Do you know him, is that it?' someone asked as she went to wash her hands.

'No,' she answered, and wished it were true.

'Does he fancy you, then?' someone else quizzed. 'Did the utterly gorgeous Enrico Ranieri hit on you in the foyer, and you did your usual thing and told him to get lost? Is that why he was so angry after you rushed off?'

Had he been angry?

'Eyes like icecaps on a volcano,' someone described.

Freya dried her hands and imagined Enrico in one of his cold rages. She'd experienced enough of them in their time together to know how they looked.

The problem with Enrico was that he was an exciting mix of hot-blooded Italian and cool sophisticate. Put him in a temper and he could go either way—ice-cold or so blisteringly hot you could fear for your skin…or other parts.

Those other parts quivered so badly Freya had to squeeze her thighs together. Stop thinking about him like that! she told herself.

'It wasn't seeing your little boy that annoyed him, was it?' The anxious question came from one of the other mothers with a child in the crèche. 'I mean, if he doesn't like children and decides to close down day care, I don't know how I…'

'Trust me, he isn't quite that archaic,' Freya heard herself say with enough tight sarcasm to make her wish she'd kept her impulsive mouth shut.

They pounced on that statement. 'You do know him!'

'No, I don't.' But her cheeks went hot.

'He stopped dead when he saw you. I was there. I saw it happen. I thought he was going to grab hold of you by the neck and strangle you.'

So did I, Freya thought with a small inner shiver. 'Sorry,' she muttered, 'but my break is over.' And she fled before they could grill her to the point that she really tripped herself up.

Damn you, Enrico, she thought as she hurried towards the bank of lifts. I hope you're pleased with yourself for stirring this up!

Enrico wasn't pleased at all. He was sprawled in a chair behind his desk, elbow resting on its arm, a long finger stroking the firm line of his mouth, eyes narrowed and glinting dangerously as he played out the image Freya had kindly placed in his head.

It wasn't as if he hadn't seen her in that position before, so it was easy for him to imagine it—though she'd usually been naked and almost always sitting there while he stood over her, enjoying the feel of her mouth around—

His groin released a spasm that funnelled right down the length of him in response to the warm, wet memory of her tasting tongue. He shot to his feet, angry—disgusted—that he could still respond so quickly to a woman who turned him so cold now.

Well, not right now, he conceded as he spun to stare out of the window while he tried to bring his libido in check.

She'd come to him so crazily innocent, she'd been shocked the first time he'd encouraged her to do that for him. By the end of their relationship she'd been so good with that sexy mouth that he had not been able to tolerate another woman doing it for him since.

'*Dio*,' he muttered. By the end, she'd been so good at a lot of things that he had barely been able to look at her without wanting her to try her newly acquired whiles out on him some more.

What he had not envisaged was her wanting to try those whiles out elsewhere—and especially not on his own cousin.

One-time cousin, Enrico grimly amended. The day he had kicked Freya out of his life, he'd kicked Luca out of it, too.

Luca, with the same dark good looks that the Ranieri family were known for, he thought cynically. He had not needed to hit on Freya when he could have had any other woman he desired.

Or was it Freya who'd hit on him?

Enrico didn't know, had refused to discuss it with either of them. All he did know was that he'd gone away on business vaguely aware that she'd not been happy about something and had promised himself he would find out what was bothering her when he got home again. What he'd found when he'd got home had finished him as a loyal cousin and as a loyal lover.

And if you want to replay old memories, he told himself cynically, then replay the one where you walked in on the two of them sprawled half-naked on your own damn bed, with her legs splayed wide and his tight, tanned backside about to make its urgent thrust home.

It was a good point in his thoughts for Freya's knock to sound at the door, he mused grimly as he turned around.

Moving back to his chair, he sat down in it before calling a cold, 'Come in.'

Freya took a deep breath before reaching for the door handle, all too aware that Enrico's PA was watching her and that he, like everyone else in this building, was wondering what was going on between her and his boss.

Her face was flushed due to her mad rush up here, eyes actually sparking with a mixture of fired-up aggression and fear. Stroking a hand over her hair in a nervous gesture at the same time as she turned the handle, she pressed her trembling lips together and stepped through the door.

The first thing to hit her was the bright light flooding into the room from all angles. The next thing to hit her was the sight of Enrico himself. He was seated behind a desk and looking exactly the same as he had done four years ago, when she'd first met him on the day he'd taken over the company she'd been working for then.

All sleek, smooth elegance and stunning good looks, wrapped around a truly rampant sex appeal. Memories flooded her of the way she'd tried so hard to appear professional and efficient back then, smiling nervously while blushing shyly and feeling generally like an awkward child in the presence of some great, awesome power.

That great, awesome power had been her first encounter with her own sexual stirrings. Until that moment she'd always laughed at friends who went all fluttery when they talked about new boyfriends and said silly things like, 'Oh, you should see him! He made me so hot I wanted to drag off my clothes!'

Well, Enrico had made her feel like that. She'd been ready to drag off her clothes for this too-gorgeous-to-be-real new boss she'd been handed like one of those gifts you did not know what to do with or how to deal with.

The same crazy sensations washed right over her now as she stood there just inside the closed door and stared down the room at his seated, undeniably sexy but intimidating bulk, and she felt hot feelings spark into life, though they had no right—not for this man, who might be an amazing lover but had proved beyond a doubt that he was good for nothing else.

Her chin went up on that final denunciation. Enrico's insides knotted as he watched it happen, felt the challenge in the gesture hit low in his gut and remain there taunting him, as he watched her toss fear and defiance at him in equal doses like some unruly employee dragged before the big boss because her work attitude was unsatisfactory.

What a joke, he thought as he studied the red flags highlighting her smooth, creamy cheeks and the ice-over-fear glazing her sea-green eyes. According to her personal records, Freya Jenson was so super-efficient it would take lies to make out she was incompetent. She was never late in, never sick and never left a minute earlier than she should do. She never moaned or complained about her frankly lousy working environment or the mindless job that she did. And she had never asked for more money, though she'd worked at Hannard's for over two years and had never been given a single pay rise.

Why, Enrico asked himself, when it was perfectly obvious from the clothes she was wearing that she barely had enough money on which to exist? Why, when he could see even from here that that unflattering knot her hair was contained in needed a pair of scissors taken to it? And he *liked* her twisting, spiraling, glorious waist-length hair.

The boy had been dressed well. His head of black curls had been carefully cut and shaped into a fashionable style, and the shoes on his feet had not looked as if they'd seen better days in a scrap bin at a charity shop.

She had a good brain in her head, but she was working here as some nonentity filing clerk hidden away in the bowels of the building, while the boy lived it up on the second floor, in a nursery to beat all nurseries complete with a wide-open terrace and a veritable array of toys and care staff to entertain him.

The child was tough and unruly—loved his mamma to death and only responded to a scolding if it came from her. The nursery staff despaired of ever gaining control of him but adored him anyway because—apparently—he could make them fall about laughing just when they believed they were in danger of killing him.

He had a sense of humour, in other words. As Fredo had reminded him he used to have, when he drove everyone insane only to win them over at the last minute by some inner instinct that turned him from obnoxious brat to clown.

And Freya loved him, this boy they had made together. Everyone knew how much she loved him. Everyone knew she was the best mother in the entire world.

But she'd still kept her son from his father. Was that the move of a loving mother?

'Come and sit down,' he instructed coldly.

'I prefer to stand,' she refused.

'Sit,' he incised and felt his blood begin to race around his system while he waited for her to deny him once more.

She didn't. It was almost a disappointment. At this precise moment he would have loved any excuse to tear her into shreds with his bare hands.

With eyes carefully lowered now she moved forwards, a reed-slender thing of five feet seven with hidden treasures lurking beneath the bad suit. Lounging there in his chair, Enrico let his eyelids sweep downwards over his eyes as he looked her over in a slow, cold study that did not reflect the burn of sexual anger taking place in his gut.

Wouldn't she just love to know that his body had not forgotten her, even if his brain had done until a few short hours ago?

The dusky pink mouth was tense, he noted, though the way she was holding it like that did not hide the revealing little tremor which told him just how frightened she was.

Good, he thought as he watched her take the chair positioned on the other side of the desk, then sit down with a stiff spine and knees pressed modestly together.

Another joke, since she had proved she was perfectly happy to open those legs for anybody.

Including his cousin.

'Do you think it is appropriate to hold a conversation with your employer via the telephone at the same time as you were relieving yourself in the lavatory?' he asked.

That brought her eyes shooting upwards. Enrico

received the full blast of her green stare. 'I explained that,' she said. 'And I had finished relieving myself, for your information,' she added. 'But it is up to you to decide if you found my call offensive.'

'Yes,' he agreed without elaborating on the single comment.

She lowered her eyes again, those golden-tipped eyelashes fluttering down against her cheeks. Something else stung inside him, the desire to run his tongue across those satin-smooth cheekbones and feel those eyelashes quiver with pleasure as he did.

She was sexually receptive from her hairline to her toenails, built for the exclusive pleasures of the flesh. Yet she was sitting here like some prim spinster schoolmistress in her ugly, ill-fitting suit and with her pinned hair, tense mouth and frosted eyes.

Liar, he wanted to say as he let the silence grow between them until she shifted restively. You are just one big, in-my-face liar, Freya Jenson.

'You demanded this meeting. So talk,' he said.

'Call Fredo off guard-watch,' she responded instantly.

'No.'

'He's worrying the children—'

A sleek dark eyebrow arched. 'My son?'

Freya stiffened. 'He is not your son.'

'Luca's, then?'

Her chin came up that bit higher, the pink mouth pushing into a stubborn pout, eyes steady when they linked with his, and she said—nothing.

Freya felt her silence spray like a million pinpricks down her front as she held his cold, narrowed stare. She hated him for asking that, but…

Dear heaven, he looked good, she found herself thinking helplessly. The silk black hair that didn't dare to curl like Nicky's did, unless it was early in the morning and he'd just woken up from a long night of loving and sleep; those dark eyes, half-lost beneath two sets of long eyelashes that gave him such a sexy, slumberous look when really he was as wide awake as a hunting shark. Then there was the mouth, hidden at the moment by the long, tanned finger he had resting along its slender width. That mouth could kill you with pleasure if you let it get close enough. It could make you lose touch with everything, but how it could make you feel!

And it could slice you into tiny pieces—or the white teeth that hid behind it could—and there was the tongue that could issue insults as effectively as it could devour you in other ways.

Her nipples pricked and she knew why they did. Just thinking about that mouth—angry or hell-bent on giving you pleasure—was enough to make her breasts respond in a greedy, tight leap of remembered bliss.

She pulled in some air. 'I work here,' she informed him. 'What happened in the foyer this lunchtime has caused a big enough sensation in this building, without Fredo standing guard at the crèche and making the gossip ten times worse.'

'He is guarding my son.'

'He is not your son.' She was going to go on repeating that until hell froze over.

'White panties or grey to match the miserable suit?' he said, making her eyes flicker in confusion. 'I only ask because you left me with this…image after your very novel telephone call,' he explained. 'White or grey

anger bouncing between them acting like a static cocoon to close them into a tight corridor of seething eye contact that sizzled and sparked and spat across the desk.

'I hope I would not be quite so crass as to say that to any woman,' he fed to her like vile-tasting poison.

It hit its spot, too, sank into her flesh and hurt.

Freya straightened up, quivering like crazy. 'Stand where I'm standing, Enrico,' she responded huskily. 'Believe me, from this side of the desk you are as crass as they come.'

With that she turned, arms folding around her as she slumped down against the edge of the desk, feeling weak and shaky now because it had all become so heated when she'd been determined to—

He moved behind her. The fine hairs across her nape tingled as she waited in the thrumming, drumming silence that had fallen to find out what he was going to do or say next.

It was annoying to feel it, but tears began pricking at her backs of her eyes and her throat. She had loved this man once, and so thoroughly she'd believed nothing he could ever do would kill that love.

Maybe it wasn't dead, she thought then as her silly, dipping, thumping heart gave a squeeze to remind her that some feeling for him was still there—like a desperately hurt and wounded love that was suddenly threatening to strangle her breath.

Bleakly she stared fixedly down at her feet. Her shoes were scuffed, she noticed inconsequentially. She'd forgotten to buff them up this morning before she left the flat. And her skirt was creased.

Unclipping a hand from beneath her other arm, she tried to smooth out the creases with fingers that trembled so badly she gave up and shoved the hand back where it had been.

He appeared on the periphery of her lowered vision. A pair of long masculine legs wrapped in the finest silk-wool mix striding with long grace across the office. His shoes weren't scuffed, she saw. That almost black suit wouldn't dare to show a crease.

'Want something?' he offered.

She heard the chink of glass and shook her head. 'I have to get back…'

'To the riveting job scanning hard copy?'

That brought her head up, dignity firing up her green eyes. 'It pays my wages, Enrico.'

'Meagre wages,' he derided. 'You earned ten times that amount when you worked for me. Josh Hannard did not know what a gem he had hiding in his basement. You could have run this place more efficiently than he did standing on your head with your hands tied behind your back.'

'You sacked me—'

'For colluding with my cousin to rob me.' He nodded. 'I remember it so well. Luca made some big mistakes in his life but that one got him caught and thrown out of the family. You were only thrown out of a job.'

And your life, Freya tagged on silently. 'Without a good reference from you I was virtually unemployable.'

He just lifted his drink to his mouth and drank. Indifferent, uncaring, cold, arrogant…

She was back to those adjectives, she realised and

heaved in a deep breath. 'I didn't do it. He set me up. I caught him with his fingers in your safe and threatened to tell the police.'

'Only threatened?' A sleek eyebrow arched cynically.

And that, Freya thought, had been her downfall. Luca was family. She'd worked and lived with Enrico long enough to know that you did not shop family to anyone, especially to the police.

Or thought she knew it.

'I decided that it was up to you to make that decision. So I went back to the apartment to wait for you to get home. He arrived drunk as a skunk. I'd just got out of the bath. He had a key he said you'd given him so he could let himself in. He was standing there in our bedroom stark naked and l-laughing at me, telling me that you'd handed me over to him because—'

'You know I don't want to hear this, so why are you saying it?' Enrico cut in coldly.

'One reason,' she said, cramming the rest of that ugly scene back down inside her. 'I have as much right as the next person to defend myself against the slur you Ranieris placed on my character.'

'But I did not listen to you then, so why do you think I will listen now?'

'Because you want something from me that you are not going to get without giving me a fair hearing and then reparation for what you and your rotten cousin did to me.'

'Are we talking about my son?'

'He isn't your son.'

The tension was heating up again. Enrico stiffened infinitesimally. 'He is my son,' he insisted.

'I want proof of that.'

'Perdono?' He stared at her. 'Isn't that my line?'

Freya crossed her arms more tightly and refused to rise to his sarcasm. 'I don't need to prove anything,' she bluffed. 'And since I don't want you to be Nicky's father I am contesting your claim. If you're that sure of yourself then prove it,' she challenged. 'I want DNA proof.'

'Is this your idea of a joke?' he demanded.

Not so she'd noticed. Freya gave a small shrug. 'I'm the woman you believe tripped like a butterfly from Ranieri to Ranieri—'

'Will you stop saying my name as if it is an insult?' he ground out.

But the name was an insult to her. 'If what you believe about me is true, then even this man-tripping butterfly would not know if you are my son's father. So I demand proof before I let you near Nicky,' she repeated.

'But anyone with eyes can tell that he belongs to me!' Enrico bit out.

'Or Luca,' she said, and watched with grim satisfaction as his handsome face locked up. 'Unless, of course, what you believe about me is just a pack of wicked lies you enjoyed swallowing…'

'I did not enjoy it,' he answered stiffly.

'Then in my place,' she continued, undeterred by the interruption, 'no caring mother would want a man who can believe such bad things about her to have anything to do with her child. Your cynical view of me would inevitably rub off on him and poison his mind about the mother he loves.'

'I would not do that.'

'I don't believe you. So I repeat, you prove Nicky is your son because I am not going to help you.'

He turned on her then, slamming the glass down. 'But you *know* he's my son!'

'Do I?'

'Stop playing this game, Freya.' He frowned impatiently. 'This is stupid. *I* know he is mine, even if you cannot be sure.'

'Oh, that was good, Enrico.' She smiled. 'I turn the tables on you and you're turning them back again—but that was a mistake,' she declared. 'Because all you've just managed to do is to confirm what a truly uncaring and cynical bastard you are. So let me put it bluntly…' Freya straightened from the desk. 'I don't want you having any influence in my son's life, therefore I will do whatever it takes to keep you out of it. I'll fight you with medical science if you make me, then I'll fight you in court.'

'You have the cash handy to back that up?'

'There is such a thing as legal aid in this country,' she pointed out. And on that she turned for the door. 'Call Fredo off,' she added as she started walking. 'Or I will inform the authorities that we have a child-stalker in the building.'

'Where the hell do you think you're going?'

Freya's head went back. 'I'm walking out of here—'

'Out of your job—?'

The challenge landed like a barb to hit dead centre of its target, acting like a lead weight that dropped at her feet and pulled her to a stop.

'No,' she whispered.

'Need it, do you, Miss Jenson?' he drawled. 'Need the meagre wages it pays into your bank?'

'Yes,' she breathed.

'Need the day care it gives to your son, also? Now, just how would you manage if it wasn't there…?'

Freya's insides began trembling, the meaning behind each single taunt making her feel suddenly very sick. Cold defiance was only effective as a weapon when you had the resources to back it up.

Enrico had just shown her that she had none.

She turned slowly. It was the only way to do it if she didn't want to collapse in a heap on the floor. He was still standing by the drinks cabinet, lounging there now like some super-arrogant modern sculptured Italian god, with his long legs crossed at the ankles and his casual air of sartorial elegance, his power and confidence knocking the spots off her attempt to gain the upper hand. The afternoon sun was pouring in through the windows, catching hold of his lean, golden features and glinting, hard eyes, and his even harder-looking mouth clipped by a tight, taunting smile.

She'd gone quite nicely pale, Enrico noted with grim satisfaction. Toss your head at me now if you dare.

'You wouldn't,' she husked out.

'Why not?' he countered. 'I am the crass bastard who hands you over to his cousin for a bit of good sex, remember? I am capable of doing anything.'

He didn't mean it, Freya told herself anxiously. He was just getting his own back on her for calling him crass. 'But it would hurt so many other mothers with—'

'Oh, come on, Freya,' he cut in, 'you worked with

me for a year so you know the score. If you wanted to cut costs at Hannard's, where would you begin—?'

'Not with the crèche!' she cried out.

'Because you have a vested interest there?' Her eyes were flashing with fear, not defiance now, Enrico noted. 'Whereas I do not.'

'You—you…' The words trailed off, bitten back before she could say them.

Enrico leant forward slightly. 'Yes?' he prompted. 'Were you about to say something important then, *cara*? Were you about to tell me that I *do* have a vested interest there?'

'No,' she choked out.

He relaxed back again. 'Your own job, then,' he moved on with a zealous, razor-like slice. 'If you had to sit on my side of the desk, what other cost-cutting exercise would you be looking at? The filing department, perhaps?' he suggested. 'That vast paper storeroom in the basement of this building that uses up expensive workspace that could be leased out to some other business for a damn good return?'

'Every business has files to store.' Her arms were back round her body again, trying to defend the panic erupting beneath their tight clasp.

'All the efficiently run businesses I know do not employ a clutch of mindless people for the exclusive task of feeding paper into a couple of ancient scanning machines,' he responded with contempt. 'I could contract out—bring in fifty people with fifty state-of-the-art machines and clear that whole basement of paper in a week. It would cost me maximum—' He named a figure that made Freya blench. 'That makes your job and the jobs of your fellow paper-scanners redundant. Now, where do I turn next to cut costs?'

Freya was really trembling now—no, shivering, her skin as cold as ice. In one easy shift of his brain he'd threatened to relieve her of her job, plus those of the dozen others who worked in the basement with her. And if that wasn't enough, he was also threatening to relieve thirty-four other mothers of their child-care facility, thereby making the staff that ran the crèche redundant, too.

'You don't deserve a son,' she breathed thickly. 'You don't deserve to be standing there at all! You should be crawling around in some gutter right now, getting your just deserts for being such an outright low-down, no-good excuse for a man!'

Impervious to insults, Enrico just shrugged a broad shoulder. 'I am in the business of saving drowning companies, not people,' he answered. 'And I can tell you bluntly that this place runs on pure fresh air right now. Everyone working here has been living on borrowed time,' he added grimly. 'There is not a single employee I would willingly keep on.'

'And I will be the first one to go,' she muttered. 'I h-hate you,' she added on a driven breath.

'Really? Now, I wonder what incentive I could find that would change your mind about that? More money, perhaps? A safer job? Child care for the *bambino* to better that which he enjoys now?'

Her green eyes sparkled at him, face so white Enrico wondered if she was about to faint. 'He loves the care he gets right here,' she insisted unsteadily.

'Come and sit down again and we will discuss it…'

But Freya didn't want to sit down. She wanted to turn around and run and never look back. Another silence stretched; so did the tension, keening like rusty wire scraping across her bones. She could feel him watching her, waiting, could feel the cold, hard, ruthless cut of his brain calculating what more it was going to take to make her give in.

'I think, Miss Jenson, this might be a good point for me to remind you of exactly who I am...'

And now he was truly pulling rank. Her spine stiffened tautly. But she still couldn't get her leaden feet to budge.

'Don't threaten me, Enrico.' She made one last husky grab at control here.

For an answer Enrico straightened up and walked back to his desk. With a smooth reach of his hand he picked up the telephone, his hard black gaze not leaving her wary, pale face.

'Carlo,' he said smoothly, 'I am terminating Miss Jenson's employment with this company, with immediate effect. Have her workstation cleared and her personal possessions brought up here, please.'

As cool as that, he completely shattered her. As cool as that, he put down the phone. 'There,' he drawled lazily, 'sacked again.'

Totally impassive, he leant back against the desk and waited for the full weight of what he had just done to sink in.

Then he said levelly, 'Now come back here and sit down...'

Like a ghost on a walkabout, Freya moved towards him. If he'd thought the cheap suit resembled grey tissue paper, then the colour of her face matched it now.

Had he seriously sacked her? Enrico asked himself. Hell, he did not know if he was serious. Could he be this ruthless to a woman in her situation? Hell, yes, he admitted, so long as he did not know her as intimately as he knew this particular woman.

Other than for that small detail, Freya knew as well as he did that you did not take personal circumstances into consideration when you worked in his line of business.

So she believed him, even if he wasn't sure he believed himself.

She came to a stop right in front of him. With the chair she'd been sitting on earlier nudging against her right knee, the stretched length of his long legs was blocking her way and preventing her from moving to sit down.

This close up he could see the fine tremors attacking her slender figure. Her eyes were lowered, her arms wrapped around her body as if they were some kind of protection.

But they were not.

'Please don't do this to me,' she whispered. 'I need this job.'

For some inexplicable reason, that shaky little plea made his body stir in a flood of heat.

Enrico let it happen.

He could smell her perfume, warm and female and tantalisingly light. The suit was a sack but it did not stop him from building an image of what lay hidden beneath: the pale, firm breasts with their wonderfully sensitive nipples, the slender ribcage that loved to be licked, just like the tiny oval of her navel and the delicate lines of her groin.

Go any lower and he was in trouble, he mused grimly, so flicked his gaze back to her face. *Bella*, he thought. *Molto bella*, even with her too-pale skin and small, trembling mouth and the hidden starkness of her green eyes.

If he took her hair down, would she resist him? If he leant over and kissed that trembling mouth, would she bite?

He had her right where he wanted her and she knew it. She was defeated in every way but for that one important confession: *yes, he's your son.* It would come sooner or later. He was not that bothered about hearing it right now because this was much more potent, this warm sensation that was seeping nicely into his blood.

Could he let himself want her like this again? Sure, a lazy voice in his head replied. You've learned very well over the last three years how to take physical pleasure without an emotional connection—a great learning curve that you could repeat on the likes of this cheating, lying, robbing, *sexy* female who, for twelve glorious months, once fulfilled your every emotional and sexual need.

For three long years he'd never been able to achieve quite that level of sexual excitement again—or give anywhere near that much of himself emotionally again.

She owed him. She owed him in so many ways that it was almost like an orgasm in itself to just stand here relishing the different ways she was about to repay the debt.

'You have something to offer me as incentive to change my mind?' he prompted softly.

She gave no answer. Her eyes remained lowered. The heat inside him began to increase.

'Yourself, maybe?' He gave her a clue as to where he was going with this. 'Perhaps you are wondering if that sensational body hidden beneath the grey sack still has the power to turn me on...'

Did it?

Freya shocked herself by actually pondering the disgusting suggestion. Would sex with him buy her back her job?

Something sizzled inside her. It was an even more shocking sensation called...temptation.

Well, fight it! she snapped at herself. Remember what this is really about: Nicky—not the humiliating price of sex!

But the atmosphere between them was really beginning to fizz the way it used to. The sudden awareness of him as a full-blooded, very physical and sexual being with the sensual touch of a—

Freya sucked in a breath, slender throat working as she tried to keep her mind on track. He's a bastard, she told herself. A true, cold-hearted, ruthless Neanderthal who thinks nothing of sacking me from my job in one sentence, then suggesting we have sex in the next!

But what could she do? What could she say to put the swine in his place? Her job was her only source of income. She depended on it as others did on water to drink. Without it she was useless as a caring provider for Nicky, totally defenceless against anything else Enrico decided to do to her to make her bend to his will.

Call his bluff—walk away—her common sense challenged her. You said it down there in the ladies' room: even Enrico could not be so archaic as to sack you because you refuse to give him what he wants.

'L'alimentazione della donna è nel suo silenzio,' he murmured softly.

A woman's power is in her silence, she translated.

Not so she'd noticed, Freya thought bitterly. She'd never felt weaker in her life.

Then he reached out to curve long fingers beneath her chin and lift it. Eyes clashed with eyes. Intimacy, familiarity licked like a flame through her insides and filled her with the knowledge of what he was going to do next.

'No,' she gasped out in shaken protest.

But too late. His dark head was already moving closer, his mouth already parting to cover hers. And it did it in that oh, so gentle, persuasive way it had always used to, before they began making love.

Response sent a tight sting running right through her middle. She tried to fight it. She kept her fingers clenched tightly beneath her arms and refused to kiss him back, even if she could not pull her mouth away.

But she could taste Enrico, the man she had loved and lost but never forgotten. He kissed her the way Enrico had always kissed her, with a slow and agonisingly sumptuous patience until the pleasure of it filled just about every sensual crevice she possessed. The gentle tip of his tongue found its way into one of those crevices, parting her lips and making her tremble as she fought the need to respond. Long fingers began sliding from her chin to her nape, and the way he tilted her head back that bit more was quite simply Enrico at his slow, seductive best.

Pull back, Freya told herself. Don't let him do this.

But she couldn't pull back. And the slow slide of his tongue across the inner tissue of her mouth was exquisite. A dizzying dip into what felt like drug-induced pleasure. Then her hair came loose to tumble free as a bird down the tension in her back and he drew her closer. The moment her front made contact with his the fight was over for her. It was as if he'd thrown a switch and turned her on like a light.

It was wrong, it was *bad*, but she still couldn't stop herself from being drawn into the kiss like a fool with no brain who couldn't pull back from the brink.

She groaned as she felt her fingers unclenching. Tense and trembling, they unwrapped themselves from around her ribcage and began feeling their way up the smooth cloth of his jacket, then continued on in a tense drift across the thin covering of his white shirt.

Enrico muttered something in soft, thick Italian, parting his thighs so he could draw her even more into the bowl of his hips—and she let him, felt his muscle-tight promise pushing against her stomach, felt its tempting, tantalising length and hardening strength cause a knock-on effect inside her, dragging at finely layered sexual muscles and sending her hips moving against him in response.

'Feeling the pull, *cara*?' he murmured against the soft moist hungry warmth of her mouth.

The slow lick of his tongue took her answer away. She released a helpless little groan instead. The fine tremors attacking her were all-knowing and wanting and uncontrollable. Reaching between their bodies, he flicked open a couple of shirt buttons, then took her hand and fed it inside. It was like being allowed to briefly touch heaven. She felt the pleasurable prickle of chest hair against her palm and the muscle-bound warmth of his golden skin. Then he was taking her other hand and feeding downwards to where he wanted it and held it there, while his long fingers stroked sensually down the length of her fingers, making wetness pool in the cup of her sex.

Enrico wondered how far he intended to take this.

All the way, was the answer he gave himself as he felt his body pumping up to meet the slow, knowing stroke of her fingers beneath the encouraging pressure of his. The thick slurry of desire was already taking him over, the need to be naked and doing this fogging out his common sense. The fine scrape of her nails against his chest was making the muscles beneath his skin quiver, and she could still kiss like a shy and tremulously eager virgin. She was warm and soft and erotically compliant, sweet-tasting and hungry but tantalisingly unsure of herself.

It was wonderful—sensationally, gloriously, gorgeously, intimately Enrico, Freya thought helplessly. She'd adored this once, loved it, learned to want more and more of what this man could make her feel. He was beautiful, so sexually expert at making her feel unbelievably special she didn't even want to stop him when she felt his fingers releasing the buttons on her jacket.

Her first chance to grab sanity came when he released her mouth so he could look down at what he'd uncovered. Dark eyelashes lay against the framework of his cheekbones as he viewed the lack of clothing beneath the thin jacket, save for a lacy white bra.

'So you could not throw all of me away.' The soft laugh he released tingled like magic across her newly exposed flesh.

Blushing like fire and angry because of it, Freya reached out to tug the jacket shut but he was there first, his kiss-moistened mouth tilted by a smile as he reached to trace the shape of the bra's scalloped edge with a feather-light finger. Her creamy smooth flesh swelled and quivered. His smile deepened as he watched it happen and the next thing she knew his thumb had slipped inside her bra and was gently circling a tingling, tightening nipple, encouraging it to spring out.

Unable to stifle a soft gasp of pleasure, Freya closed her eyes and whispered helplessly, 'Oh, please, don't do this to me.'

'Sex with your first lover is a life-long aphrodisiac, *cara mia*,' he murmured huskily. 'Old and withered, if I walked into a room with you in it, I would still make you feel like this.'

'But I don't want to!'

'I know,' he laughed harshly, then licked her small sob away. 'It is what makes this so exciting.'

Glancing at his face, she saw that the flush of passion written across it was spoiled by the glint of anger burning in his eyes. He wanted her like crazy—but he was still hating her like crazy.

And didn't she hate him the same way?

Yes, she told herself. *Yes*! So what are you doing here?

About to have sex like the cheap tart he believes you to be, she answered her own question.

One kiss and you're any man's.

Sanity returned with a shuddering thump. 'Let go of me,' she breathed in utter skin-crawling horror.

His hands sprang away from her in a mocking gesture of compliance. The fact that her hands still possessed his chest and the hard ridge of his penis made her shudder some more as she stepped back from him, snaking her fingers away at the same time.

She felt pale and icy but looked hot and flushed. Her jacket was hanging open and her breasts were no longer seated in her lacy bra cups. Two tight nipples were pointing defiantly up at her and she had never, ever despised herself as much as she did just then as she pushed her taunting breasts away while he just leant there, arms folded across his front now, watching her without giving a care to the fact that his own arousal was still lying tight along the zip of his trousers.

'I hate you,' she whispered.

'So you keep saying.'

'I want to kill you!'

'But then that would leave our son without a father,' he smoothly pointed out.

Freya stilled, fingers clutching the edges of her jacket, which she had been about to yank shut. Head lowered, eyes frozen by a silence that, this time, she could not bring herself to break with the denial that stung the tip of her kiss-swollen tongue.

'Ah, we make progress,' Enrico drawled lazily, unable, while she was still frozen, to stop his eyes from following the warm tide of silk red hair flowing around her shoulders and her arms.

Unutterably exquisite, he observed grimly, even with split ends in need of attention. She always had been the most delicious and exciting package he'd ever had the pleasure of unwrapping, whether from workaday

clothes, leisure-wear or sexy, very expensive gowns.
Pinned up, tucked in, shapeless or just plain ugly, unwrapping Freya Jenson was a man's kind of pleasure he
had wanted to keep all to himself.

Then along had come Luca.

'Found your conscience at last, *cara*?' he taunted on
the back of that final reminder. 'Thinking about all those
poor people out there you will put out of work along
with yourself if you don't learn to curb your lying
tongue?'

She heaved in a breath. 'Nicky is—'

'Nicolo Alessandro Valentino Jenson,' he inserted
with the silky dark luxury of his Italian accent. 'You just
could not resist naming my son after me...'

CHAPTER FOUR

HE WAS right. Freya went hot all over. Enrico got his Christian name from his paternal grandfather, Alessandro from his maternal one. Valentino had been the name of his late father. Nicolo was exclusive to Enrico himself.

'Nicolas,' she corrected.

'In defiance,' he nodded. 'You are a hard woman, Freya Jenson, with a hard heart and a taste for vendetta. But when it came right down to it you could not stop yourself from naming *our* child for his father.'

What did she say? Did she give in now? Did she swallow her anger and bitterness and pride and give this man who'd let her down so badly the triumph over her he was waiting for?

'If you want me to say it out loud then I won't— ever.' Because even now, with all his threats laid out in front of her, she still could not give him that much.

'Although it is the truth? He is my son?'

Lips pinned tightly together, she said nothing.

'Rumour has it that Luca is so vain in the bedroom, he can only perform if there is a mirror in which he can see himself,' Enrico's hateful voice resonated on. 'There was no such mirror in our bedroom, *cara*, so the chances are that he could not have kept it up long enough to have been any good at the seed-sowing stuff. Unless you held a hand mirror over your face while he did it, of course.'

Freya hit him. She did not know where the impulse had come from, or why it had taken that particular nasty taunt to make her react the way she did, but the next thing she knew her fingers were leaving red score marks on his hard, handsome cheek.

'S-sorry,' she heard herself stammer. 'But you—'

Too late once again. The black eyes flared up with rage and his hands snaked out. Next thing, he'd hauled her back against him. His mouth this time was hard and cruel. In the few seconds it took between her slap, his flare of rage and their kiss, Freya had run the gauntlet of shock, dismay, then fear and arrived at passion, which was unleashed from its restraints and hell-bent on devouring both of them. There was no sensual patience now, but the full onslaught of a grinding mouth-to-mouth possession that made her jaw ache and her lips burn with its heat.

She wriggled and squirmed and grabbed at his hair to pull his head away but it didn't stop anything, in fact, it only made things worse. He deepened the kiss and hot need flooded her. Her tugging fingers curled then clung. It was like giving the green light to an orgy of the senses. Anger fed it, aided by the stinging echo of the slap. They'd had fights before which had ended up wallowing in hot, seething passion—but never, ever anything as hot and seething as this.

It was almost as if her brain had shut off—but it hadn't. She was aware of everything, knew what she was doing was wrong…stupid! But he felt and sounded and tasted so good! All man-out-of-control and fast, breathtaking hunger. She fed him and urged him on. Her jacket was wrenched from her arms and her shoulders. It landed somewhere in a limp grey heap. Her bra went next and he did not release her mouth even as his own jacket was raked off his back and flung aside.

A new kind of heat trammelled up inside her, the kind that set her gasping as she wrenched free the rest of his shirt buttons while he pushed up her skirt to close his hands round her thighs. The slide of those knowing fingers from lace-top hold-ups to lacy panties made her gasp and quiver. When he found what he was hunting for, the finger he ran along the groove of stretched fabric between her legs set fine, receptive tissue unfurling in helpless, pulsating arousal, and the way that finger trembled as he hooked the fabric out of his way only made her gasp and quiver again.

It had been the memory of the warm, slick, knowing stroke of his finger that had awoken her in the middle of the night, aching and throbbing with need, only to find herself alone in her bed. It had been the pleasure-giving feel of that finger sliding inside her that she'd yearned for so badly in those lonely moments, and the only way to relieve the agony had been to curl into a tight ball and sob her heart out.

Now it was here. It was real and she'd never felt so desperate.

'You're hot for me,' he rasped out, though his voice shook as he said it.

Tugging her mouth free, she opened her eyes and found herself looking into two deep, dark pits of angry derision that were spiked by pure, untamed, passionate want.

'Do I stop?' he demanded.

Her reply was a shrill little whimper.

'Do I—?' he raked at her.

'No!' she sobbed out.

Fire lit those dark, deriding eyes with triumph. She heard the scrape of a zip and her sexual temperature went soaring. When he lifted her up to straddle him with her knees pressed into the desk either side of his hips, she arched her lower body into him and clung. The heated clash of skin against skin made her wild and wanting. By now his head was drawn back on his neck, her fingers buried in his hair to hold him there while she helped him maintain their hot-tongued, deep, deep kiss. Then, with a single hard move, he used his hands on her hips to position her above him and draw her down onto the long, hard length of his waiting shaft.

It was like sheathing himself in satin fire. Enrico had to close his eyes on a shuddering groan as pure pleasure flooded through him in a heated rush. When he opened his eyes again, her pointed breasts taunted his tongue and he shifted his hands to support her back so she could arch further and give him access.

They'd made love in some outlandish places. They'd fallen on each other like wild animals often enough. But never like this before, in his office, in broad daylight, on a desk, with their clothes half off and their bodies driven by the concentrated power of driving, angry, deep-thrusting lust.

Deserting her breasts, he went for her mouth again, greedy for everything at once. He despised her, but he had never felt more alive than he was feeling at this moment. The power of it drenched him in the burning heat of sensual excess. She was the one causing the mayhem, her slender hips moving up and down on him and rotating in the way he had taught her in order to enhance their every pleasure.

She was amazing at it. He lifted his mouth away from hers to look at her. Her eyes were so dark now, the green in them was lost. He held her gaze. It was part of the excitement to have their eyes and bodies locked, as her hands clung to his hair. Her own hair hung like a crackling curtain that cloaked both of them while his long fingers moulded her slender, tight-skinned hips as she rode him, greedily taking every bit of him in her sliding, taut-muscled, sensuous sheath.

'Coming, *amore*?' he husked as he felt her first telling ripples take hold of him. 'Want to fly with your lover?'

'Yes,' she gasped.

He stabbed. She cried out. He picked her up by her clinging hips and backed her up against the nearest wall and took control with a hard, angry thrust that drove her so mindless she cried out his name as she came in a gasping, clenching, pulsing flood all around him.

His name, he thought angrily. *His!* And then he followed this flowing-haired witch into the drumming, hot space of sensual heaven.

Or hell, he amended a few seconds later when the storm was over.

For where or how with anyone else was he ever going to match that?

When had he ever matched it since she'd gone from his life?

Her head was resting now on his shoulder, her hair splayed over both of them. She was shivering and quivering and as weak as a kitten.

And his own legs were not so steady, especially when he made the grim decision to withdraw.

Her legs slithered down the length of his. If tension had a taste to it, then it would be of the aftermath of sex with a woman you should not have indulged with.

Now it was over he was regretting it to the tips of his tingling, clenched, still-pumping nerve ends.

He took a step back and began straightening his clothing. Freya had to lean weakly back against the wall behind her, eyes tight shut, breathing nearly stopped.

'*Dio,*' Enrico muttered to himself when he saw how badly his fingers were trembling, and strode off to the adjoining bathroom, where he spent a few minutes sluicing his face and trying to calm himself.

He should not have done that. What the hell had he thought he'd been playing at?

Fastening his shirt buttons, he actually felt himself blush when he saw that his dark silk tie was still knotted around his throat.

Good definition of crass, Ranieri, he told himself grimly.

By the time he let himself out of the bathroom, Freya was standing over her discarded clothes with her naked back to him, fumbling with shaking fingers in her efforts to fasten her bra.

So what now? he wondered, and didn't have an

answer. On a low sigh he shoved his hands into his trouser pockets and leant a shoulder against the wall while he watched her twist the bra around then shimmy into it. Her skirt had fallen back into place by its own volition but he found himself wondering what her panties were doing beneath it.

Lace bra, panties and lace-topped hold-up stockings. His mouth shifted into a grimace as he watched her stoop to gather up her jacket. It was dragged around her body like a piece of sackcloth. Her hair was caught inside it and his fingers twitched in his pockets with the need to go and set it free.

She did that, yanking out the long, silken swathe with a brutality that made Enrico wince. And the silence between them was so thick now you could barely breathe.

Her bag was lying on the floor by the chair with its contents spilling out from it. She must have forgotten to close the clasp when she'd rushed out of the ladies' room, Freya realised, and vaguely wondered how she was going to bend down there and scoop it all back in when her stomach was dipping and diving so badly she would probably end up slumped on the floor in a puddle of dizzying shame.

How could she have done that? Let him do *that* to her?

He'd done it.

Through that same oddly vague haze, she watched Enrico walk to the chair then squat to pick up her overlarge, cheap, imitation-leather bag and begin to gather its contents with long, steady fingers that had just…

She sucked the breath into her lungs like a drowning person suddenly finding air to breathe. He heard it happen, but went on still with what he was doing, his dark head lowered, a bright red toy Ferrari held in his hand.

Nicky's toy Ferrari.

Her son's little toy car.

Enrico owned several Ferraris—collectors' pieces most of them—only they were the man-sized real thing.

'You want me to say something,' he gritted.

'No,' she responded with a quaver that told her the tears were not far away.

While she had been behaving like a whore, her son was being safely taken care of by specialised staff six floors beneath her guilty, disgusted, trembling feet.

And she didn't even have a right to be in this building any more. Neither did Nicky.

They'd both been terminated by the ruthless, heart-less seducer of weak-willed, easy females. The man with—

A knock sounded at the door. Freya had this sudden, wildly hysterical image of Security arriving to escort her out.

Enrico straightened abruptly, tossing her bag onto the desktop—the same desktop where she'd—

'Wait,' he called out in terse command to whoever was on the other side of the door. He picked up his jacket and shrugged it back on.

Six-feet-three, dark and too good-looking for his own good, recently ravished, yet he didn't have a hair out of place or a single crease in his clothes, Freya noticed. Did his legs feel hollow the way hers did? Was he suffoca-ting beneath the same thick, clammy blanket of shame?

He turned then to look at her—no, not to look

exactly, but to flick a pair of grimly half-hooded eyes over her ashen face, then her limp and dishevelled suit. In all her life Freya had never fought back her tears as fiercely as she had to do at this precise moment.

Her mobile phone began to ring. Forcing her unsteady legs to move, she went towards Enrico, hoping to goodness he moved out of her way so that she could get at her bag without her having to brush against him.

'Leave it,' he said in a sandpaper rasp that scored across her skin.

She stepped between him and the chair. 'I can't,' she shook out.

Her phone only rang in emergencies.

'Now, don't go into one of your panics,' Cindy, the crèche manager, warned quickly, 'but Nicky's had a fall. He was showing off for the gorilla and…'

The rest was said to fresh air. Freya just dropped the phone and ran.

'What, for *Dio's* sake?' Enrico called after her.

But she was already pulling open the door. Enrico's PA stood on the other side of it holding a cardboard box and blocking her way. Freya vaguely recognised her own things stacked inside the box and, on a whimper that had nothing to do with the physical reminder that she'd been sacked, but with a need to get past the cold-eyed young man, she shoved him inelegantly out of the way and raced for the lifts with her hair flying out behind her and no shoes on her feet.

No damn shoes! Enrico saw as he went after her. Where the hell were her shoes?

'Move, Carlo,' he gritted as his PA was only just recovering from Freya's rude push.

This time Carlo managed to step to one side before the more heavily built Enrico threatened to knock him over, staring after him as his boss took off at a run.

Enrico didn't run; Enrico *strode* through with arrogant elegance. He did not chase after women; women chased after him.

But Enrico was not an idiot. He'd worked it out that if Freya was running it had to have something to do with their son.

Their son!

It hit him for the first time what those words truly meant to him. Something hard like iron congealed in his gut. He reached the lifts just as the doors were closing with Freya on the other side of them.

Cursing beneath his breath, he stabbed the call button for another ride. It arrived within seconds and he strode out onto the second floor in time to follow the stream of wild, red-silk hair and found himself striding into a large, brightly coloured room.

Freya scanned the room at the speed of lightning, passing over the paint corner, the rest corner, the small sea of children busy doing the things that small children do, until she found her son in the climbing corner.

Of course the climbing corner, she thought with a barely stifled choke. Where else would Nicky be showing off for Fredo?

And who else would be squatting there, holding her son firmly in his big arms? Nicky was curled there as if it was his only source of comfort, his dark head tucked into Fredo's shoulder, his little arms wrapped tightly round the big man's neck.

Fredo looked up as she approached them. For a tough

bruiser he looked very pale. Cindy was squatting down beside them and trying to get Nicky to let her see his face.

'He's fine—honestly,' she said quickly to Freya. 'He took a tumble off the climbing blocks and would have landed safely on the cushion floor, only he managed to bump his cheek on the way. But, as usual, he won't let me look at the damage.'

Oh, the indignity of it, Freya thought helplessly as she came down beside Fredo. 'Come on, big boy,' she encouraged with only a tiny shake to her voice. 'Let Mummy take a look.'

'No.' Nicky's arms tightened around Fredo.

'He hurt his pride more than himself,' Fredo said gruffly.

'I know,' Freya replied without removing her eyes from her son.

If she had done so she would have seen the way Cindy was staring at her, at the wild flow of her hair streaming down to her waist, then at the tall guy who'd come to stand right behind her. He was looking down at Nicky wrapped in the gorilla's arms. The newcomer just had to be Enrico Ranieri, Cindy realised. And if those ink-black eyes were not Nicky's eyes, then she was the dumb blonde some people took her for.

'Sorry, boss,' Fredo said huskily. 'I could not reach him quickly enough to break his fall.'

That was the point when Freya became aware of Enrico, then she caught the look on Cindy's face. Heat poured into her cheeks and she quickly fluttered her eyes back to Nicky, hands, arms trembling as she reached out for him and gently untangled the small boy. Nicky transferred his arms to her neck, little fingers curling in her hair as she stood up with him and, ignoring everyone else, walked over to another corner of the room where it was quiet, and sat down on a bench with him straddling her lap.

There was a calm, gentle dignity in the way she coaxed Nicky out of hiding to show her the damage. Enrico watched, his expression grave, his insides locked in some strange, aching place that made him feel so separate from all of this that he struggled to understand why he was here at all.

He knew nothing about children, even less about brightly coloured playrooms like this. He was used to smart, efficient offices and slick business environments, living spaces made up of neutral-coloured elegance and hushed sophistication, not bright primary colours, noise and mess.

He was even used to fluffy blue-eyed blondes staring at him, but this one did it in a way that made him want to run a finger under his shirt collar like a nervous boy.

She knew. She'd seen the likeness between father and son. He could sense it, even though he refused to let himself check that out by looking directly at her.

And over there was his two-year-old son, who did not know him from a stranger. Plus an ex-lover he did not want as a lover again, yet he had just sunk himself into her like a man with a fever and no damn finesse.

Look at her, he told himself. She was sitting there with that hair like fire all around her, pale and strained-looking. But smiling tenderly as she inspected the child's face while he stroked his hands over that glorious hair and listened intently to what she was saying to him.

Hot nymph and earth mother in one package.

In the last short hour he had coolly put her out of work and hotly ravished her, but there she sat, looking as serene as an angel as she talked to his son.

His son! It was finally—*finally*—getting through to him. He had been repeating those words to himself since he'd first seen the boy in the foyer. But it was only now as he stood here in this alien place with yet another clutch of curious eyes fixed upon him that the full power of those words truly took shape.

He had to go over there, he knew that he did. He could not let the moment pass by. He had to make his first approach towards that small person as a father, with all of these strangers looking on. His fingers curled into fists at his sides and it was only as they did so that he felt something in his right palm.

He looked down, then just stared at the red toy Ferrari. It was the same model he'd used to drive around in when Freya was in his life.

In every which way he happened to stumble upon, she had been making connections between him and that little boy; consciously or subconsciously—it did not matter.

And, for some crazy reason, he realised this knowledge was causing a rare burn to attack the back of his throat. He swallowed, glanced at Fredo, who was looking back at him. This man, whom he had known since they were boys, could read him like an open book.

Just as he could also read Fredo, when those grave, knowing eyes gave a flick towards Freya and the child. Get over there, the look said.

He didn't want to.

He kept a dozen multimillion-dollar companies with

who knew how many employees functioning to his express bidding, yet the idea of approaching this small boy was completely defeating him.

What if Nicky was Luca's son, and he'd spent the afternoon making a big fool of himself? Threats, blackmail and intimidation could make a woman in Freya's situation say anything—lie, if she believed it was her only way out!

But she had not lied. She still had not declared anything, even when she'd finally accepted it was her only way out.

Because she was punishing him, or because she could not bring herself to lie about the father of her son?

He made himself walk on feet made of concrete, the sting in his throat dying down to be replaced by a dull throb in his gut. The fluffy blonde crèche manager was just standing there watching him like some wise, all-knowing, blue-eyed owl, but she did not know about Luca, did she?

His jaw took on a rigid clench.

Freya saw those muscles in his face tighten as he came towards them, and wondered heavily what was going through his head now.

Having second thoughts, Mr Ranieri? she mocked silently. Wondering at last if you want to be an instant father to a two-year-old boy?

Or has Luca raised his head in your nasty thoughts again?

She lowered her eyes to Nicky before her face decided to show the bitterness she was feeling inside. Nicky would not understand her expression.

'Hey,' she said as lightly as she could do in the circumstances. 'Have you noticed, by any chance, that I came running here without putting on my shoes?'

He looked down at her feet then back at her face. Freya sent him a grimace, and his solemn little face broke into one of those wonderful, white-toothed grins.

'Trust you to find it funny that I came skidding over here in my stockings just to give you a cuddle.'

She kissed the tiny bruise on his cheek as Enrico's long shadow crawled up Nicky's back then over her face.

Freya fought down the urge to shiver. Tension zapped every nerve in her back. She looked up, defiant and defensive. This was one confrontation she was not looking forward to—the one where father and son came truly face-to-face.

'He is hurt?' Enrico enquired stiffly. 'He requires professional medical attention?'

His accent had thickened, Freya noticed. His desire to be anywhere else but here right now was alive in the muscle-tense set of his whole frame.

She shook her head, having to swallow before she could bring herself to say lightly to Nicky, 'Just a bump, hmm, kiddo? We don't need an ambulance with screeching sirens or a couple of fire engines for escorts, do we?'

'No, silly,' he laughed.

Then Nicky looked up at Enrico's long, lean, sharp-suited form until he reached his severely defended face. Freya's heart gave a lurch that turned into a mammoth, throbbing ache as she watched Nicky's expression grow wary in response.

It could not go on, she realised right there in that moment. She just could not let it happen. Her own bitterness towards Enrico was something she had to deal with, but she would have to be the worst kind of mother if she let it spill over and ruin this so-important moment for her son.

Because there was only one way she could think to do this, she tipped Nicky off her knee and stood up herself, going to stand protectively behind him as she turned them both to fully face Enrico.

Then she took a deep breath. 'Nicky, darling, I want you to…'

Yet again she was too late. When your timing is out it stays out, she thought helplessly as she watched the way father and son were looking at each other and her words were swallowed when she saw the same almost unholy flare of possession light Enrico's face as it had done in the foyer.

It was there, he could see it. What had his brain been playing at, taunting himself with his cousin?

His son—*his*, not Luca's!

He could feel it again in those ink-black eyes that were connecting with him like tiny fingers reaching inside him and closing round his heart.

He just did not know what to do next.

No one had told him that life was always going to be easy, he thought helplessly. But neither had anyone bothered to whisper in his ear, 'Hey, watch out for the moment someone rips your guts out in public and hangs them out to dry.'

This moment was doing that. He just stood there and let it happen—let this miniature image of himself look him over as if he were some kind of alien from outer space. He knew he looked formidable because he *felt* formidable. He knew he should have been doing something like softening his expression and attempting to make some kind of gesture of friendliness.

But—what?

And people were watching—all of them, curious kids and adults alike.

He doesn't like children, they were thinking. Hell, look at him, he can't even bring himself to smile!

Then Freya's fingers arrived on that pair of narrow, childish shoulders, and he knew that he had to do something. His time was up. She was going to withdraw the boy from his sight.

He dropped onto his haunches, heart thundering like crazy. *'Ciao,'* he heard himself utter in a husky rasp across his constricted throat.

Why in Italian—*why*? he asked himself.

He received no answer. Something thick was gathering inside him. In a helpless, useless kind of gesture he lifted up his hand and opened it up.

The boy looked down at the red toy Ferrari car, then back at him. 'Mine?' he asked.

Enrico nodded, wanted to swallow but would not let himself. *'Vostro,'* he confirmed—again in Italian, but he was thinking in English.

It did not make any sense.

The noisy, garishly painted playroom was so silent you could have heard a pin drop. Every word he spoke was echoing like mad.

A tiny hand reached out and tentatively plucked the car from his palm. Then the little boy smiled.

It was Enrico's own smile. He was looking into his own eyes and seeing his own smile and…

His hand moved of its own volition, reaching out to run gentle fingers through the boy's glossy dark curls. It was like touching his own hair. When his fingers moved to lightly stroke the small bruise on the boys cheek, it felt so familiar it was like touching his own skin.

He could not help it. He placed his hands on Nicky's shoulders and drew the little boy towards him, breaking the protective link with his mamma, so he could brush that bruise, then the Cupid's mouth with a kiss.

A father's kiss. His heart turned over and squeezed tightly.

An Italian father's naturally tactile greeting to his son.

He could sense Freya fighting the tears as she watched them. He could sense how alert she was in case their son took exception to being touched and kissed by this man who was a stranger to him.

But they were not strangers. Even the confused and frowning two-year-old was feeling something—like a son's recognition of his own flesh and blood?

Then Nicky reached out to touch Enrico's hair with tentative fingers, mimicking him as he moved his small fingers on to touch a razor-edged cheek.

Tears gathered strength. Freya couldn't stop them. Hurt gathered with them—a mother's hurt because, until this moment, only she'd earned that engrossed expression now placed on her son's little face.

Was she jealous?

Yes, she was jealous. And desperately afraid of what this was going to mean.

Then Enrico grinned. It was the same grin Nicky had just shown to her. It wiped the austerity from his countenance.

Nicky grinned back.

Then, without any warning that he was going to do it, the little boy turned, twisting out from beneath his father's light clasp, and was taking off at a run.

That was it.

That was it!

The sum total response from son to father, before the child ran off to play with his friends.

Enrico rose to his full height, aware of the curious eyes still on him, more aware that Freya was close to tears. He glanced at Fredo, who was just looking at him, flicked his eyes to the fluffy blonde, who, by the look in her narrowed blue eyes, was not sure whether to be impressed or just plain sceptical about what she had just seen.

Well, keep watching, *cara*, because this is not over, Enrico thought grimly, and shifted his attention back to Freya. His next move was instinctive, the same instinct which helped keep him forever one step ahead of his business competitors. At this moment it was all he had left to function with.

Reaching for her shoulders, he drew Freya towards him in the same way he had done with his son. Only this was different. This was grimly measured as he lowered his dark head and placed his lips close to her ear.

'He is mine,' he husked, 'and your fate is now sealed.'

As he straightened up again she was quivering, fingers locked together in a tight clasp at her front. He looked nowhere else but at her pale face with its hidden eyes and its soft, kiss-swollen, trembling mouth.

'You have ten minutes to say your farewells here and

collect our son, *mi amore*,' he announced huskily enough to sound intimate but loudly enough for all to hear. 'Time is short and we have our wedding to organise before we leave for Milan.'

Then he kissed her full on her gasping, trembling, totally shocked mouth before turning and striding away.

CHAPTER FIVE

FREYA paused outside Enrico's office, trying desperately to keep it together until she had finished this.

The personal assistant was not around, thank goodness. Nicky was safely where he always was at this time of day—in the crèche—with Fredo standing guard and Cindy now sucking up to him because curiosity had overcome her gorilla-alarm.

Freya's mouth twisted. Tense and pale now, not kiss-swollen and tremulous. She'd overrun her ten-minute deadline by a good fifteen, because it had taken the full ten to field all the eager questions from those in the crèche who'd overheard what Enrico had said. And, while she'd played it cool and had been blushingly evasive, anger had been steadily growing inside her until she'd been ready to tear Enrico limb from limb.

Until she'd reached this door, that was. All the way through the crèche inquisition, she'd let the anger grow inside her. All the way through her eventual escape, and then the minutes she'd spent in the nearest ladies' room attempting to make herself look and feel respectable again.

Feeling respectable again had been the most difficult

part to grasp. After the use of a comb, her hair was back up in a scalp-stinging tight knot and secured by a couple of elastic bands filched from Cindy.

It was the moment when Cindy had gently pointed out that her jacket buttons were done up in the wrong order that had really thrown her.

She'd known then that they all knew what she'd been doing to get into such a dishevelled state. Or they thought they knew. She could only hope that their imaginations did not stretch as far as the real, unfettered, lustful, shameful truth.

Whatever. It would be all over the building by now—everything, from the juicy arrival of the shoeless Freya Jenson into the crèche with her hair wild about her shoulders and her jacket wrongly buttoned up, to the following entrance of the super-elegant Enrico Ranieri, looking as tall, dark and handsome and dauntingly formidable as his reputation said he was.

She could almost hear the squeals of scandalous delight shrilling down telephones lines and across e-mails as their witnesses relayed, 'She looked ravished! And guess who did the ravishing? Our gorgeous new boss! Would you believe he's Nicky's father? Would you believe they're getting married? Fast worker, hmm? I wish my shoes were hiding wherever her shoes are hiding…'

Freya wanted to shrivel up and die.

Now here she stood, about to face her persecutor and it had only just hit her that she had nothing to face him with. In just a few short hours he'd ripped her life apart and left her without a single weapon with which to fight.

Except for one…

Her top teeth buried themselves in her bottom lip. The mere hint that she could tell Enrico such a big, wicked lie was enough to make her cringe inside.

If she was wicked enough to claim that Nicky was Luca's son, would it gain her anything other than the knowledge that she had landed one hit back at him?

She couldn't do it. She only had to recall those few heart-wrenching moments down in the crèche when Nicky had connected with Enrico to know she could no more murder that special moment than she could do away with her beautiful son.

The door suddenly swung open. Freya blinked as Enrico filled the gap. An instant, uncontrollable rush of sexual awareness ran right down through her.

'If you stand there fighting with yourself for much longer you will take root,' he mocked acidly.

'But how did you—?'

'Instinct,' he clipped. 'I could feel the vibrations of your angst reaching out to me through the solid wood.'

He stepped to one side in a grim indication for her to enter. She did so reluctantly and couldn't control the small wince as she heard the door shut.

It was like revisiting the scene of a dreadful crime, she thought hollowly as she stared at the room where less than an hour ago she'd…

'Take your hair down.'

'No…' She turned to look at him as he went past her on the way to the desk. Sitting on top of it was the box containing her personal stuff with her handbag beside it. Standing alongside was a zipped-up business case which had to contain Enrico's laptop. On the floor by the chair, set neatly together, were her shoes.

He was ready to leave here.

He'd only been waiting for her to turn up.

Then what?

A trip to the nearest register office, then ten years or so of marital punishment until Nicky was old enough to cope without her around?

Freya's stomach knotted. 'Enrico…' she murmured.

'Shoes.' He indicated with a flip of a hand as if it was perfectly normal to have a pair of women's shoes standing neatly to attention by the chair.

'Listen first,' she insisted. 'A-about Nicky…'

'I'm a step ahead of you, Freya, so don't bother to say it,' he cut in yet again.

'You can't know what I was going to say!' she snapped out.

'You were about to tell yet another lie and claim that Luca is Nicolo's father.'

Freya's mouth opened and closed on a soundless gasp.

'It is what you spent five minutes struggling with outside my door,' he added.

How could he have known she'd been fighting with that? 'I w-wasn't going to say that.'

'Another lie.' He looked at her grimly. 'But, as I've told you once already today, I now *know* I am that boy's father and your fate is sealed. Now, put on your shoes so we can leave.'

'It takes more than a sperm head to make you a father,' she sliced at him.

'It also takes the opportunity to become one. You did not give me that.'

About to push her feet into her shoes, Freya lifted her head and stared at him. 'Are you daring to say that it's my fault you did not get the chance?'

'You could have called me,' he muttered. 'Once he was born and you could see for yourself that I—'

'You expected *me* to call you up and beg you to come and check Nicky out?'

'It would have cost you nothing.'

Freya laughed—cost her nothing? 'I might have been a naïve little fool when I met you, Enrico, but I'm a hell of a quick learner. What you taught me about humiliation is now seared forever into my brain! I hate you for teaching me to feel like that, do you know that?' she flashed. 'I hate you so much for it that even being in the same room as you makes me want to tear down the walls to get out!'

'The door requires less energy,' he said smoothly. 'Put your shoes on and we will use it.'

'When—' she ignored that '—did *you* make any attempt to contact *me*? I still live in the same flat I leased before I met you; you know that I kept on paying the rent even though I moved in with you. It still has the same telephone number. I don't recall finding you standing at my door enquiring after me or my child. I don't remember any telephone messages enquiring if I was OK! I *do* recall pacing the delivery suite at the hospital,' she continued furiously, 'and, between contractions, spotting a nice, glossy magazine sitting on a table filled with pictures of you with your latest conquest attached to your hip!'

He frowned. 'Was the pain very bad?'

'Did the lush brunette come through with the goods?' His frown deepened.

'Does it please you to know that while I was giving birth to Nicky you were probably enjoying yourself with that woman?'

'No,' he said gruffly. 'It does not please me.'

'I think those very helpful glossies placed you with a sexy blonde, while I was placing the floor every night because Nicky was teething,' she went on. 'Maybe you think I should have interrupted you with a phone call then, to come and see if you fancied becoming a father to my son.'

'Stop scoring points off me,' he snapped out. 'Do you think it has been easy for me to find out I have a two-year-old child?'

'He's not yours.' She just could not stop herself from saying it.

Enrico let the air leave his lungs with an angry hiss and stepped up to her to take a grip on her shoulders. 'He is mine, you vindictive witch,' he sliced into her. 'You know he is mine. I know he is mine!'

'If he didn't look so much like you, you wouldn't even be thinking that!'

He dropped his hands from her, lean body twisting away because he knew she was only telling the truth. In the thrumming silence which followed, Freya fought the tears back while she stuffed her feet into her shoes.

'Please leave us alone,' she pushed huskily into the silence. 'This marriage thing you've come up with is just a knee-jerk reaction. You know you don't want me back in your life.'

He turned, lean face hard like granite again. 'I want my son. You come with him. Marriage comes with the whole damn package.'

'Nicky is…'

'Mine,' he stated. 'You *know* it. I *feel* it. Nicolo *feels* it. We connected. I will not disconnect simply because you wish I would.'

'And I won't marry you.'

'Then I will do this the hard way and I *will* fight you through the courts. And I will win, Freya,' he warned harshly. 'For what can a jobless single mother offer the boy in comparison with what I can?'

Love, she wanted to say, but even as the word settled on the tip of her tongue she could see the ferocity of his love for Nicky burning bright in Enrico's eyes.

He loved him already! She wanted to sit down and sob her heart out.

What she actually did was lower her head and pick up her bag without saying another word.

With that grim, thick silence crowding around them, Enrico picked up the box with her belongings in it and his business case, then strode over to open the door. The PA was back at his desk, face poker-straight.

'Call Fredo and tell him to meet us at the car with our son,' Enrico instructed.

Freya lifted an anxious face to his. 'I don't think…'

'On second thoughts, leave the call to me,' Enrico amended, and turned to hand his business case to Freya so he could hunt in his jacket pocket for his mobile phone.

She felt strange, oddly detached from reality as she walked beside him towards the lifts, listening to Enrico's deep voice speaking in smooth Italian while she carried his business case as she'd used to.

He was asking Fredo if he thought Nicky would

come away with him, his fatherly instincts already beginning to work.

Jobless, he'd called her. Jobless might not make her completely powerless against a man like him in the long term, but in the short term it made her feel scared to death. How were she and Nicky going to survive without a regular wage coming in?

No crèche in which to safely leave him while she job-hunted. No money to spare for trips to see the monkeys at the zoo. Then there was rent to pay, food and utility bills to cover. She'd always managed to steer clear of unemployment benefits or Social Services' help, because she'd always known the first question they would ask her was, who is Nicky's father? Which meant that the Child Support Agency was out of the question, too. And look at him, she told herself in despair—standing next to her at the lifts and looking from his sleek head to his hand-stitched shoes like the billion-dollar man he was. Explain him away, then beg for a state handout. Admit it to them that yes, this guy is Nicky's father, but I don't want him to know that, and they would laugh in her face!

Enrico suddenly turned his back on her and paced away with the phone still stuck to his ear, his voice now low and impatient, his Italian too fast for her to translate. A lift arrived but he was already halfway back down the corridor, lean, lithe, packed with all that restless grace and elegance and switched-on sex appeal that made just looking at him stifle the breath in her throat.

As if the day hadn't thrown out enough lousy twists at her, it decided now to throw out an image of her sinking into him like a sex-starved wanton.

She turned away, despising herself for being such an easy, willing kill. Had he lost any of his dignity? Not this man. But she'd lost everything: grace, dignity, self-respect.

The lift doors had closed. She hadn't noticed. With an impatient finger she stabbed the button to call up another one. Tears stung her eyes and clogged her throat.

He arrived back at her side, and he'd switched to speaking English. She realised that he was speaking to Cindy, telling her what was about to happen in precise and cool boss-like language, then he was holding the phone out to her.

'She requires your confirmation that Nicky can leave here with Fredo.'

The word *Nicky* slid strangely off his tongue; it was kind of foreign to him yet intimate. Her stomach muscles knotted while at the same time her voice remained level and calm as she gave the permission Cindy required. A new lift arrived and they entered it as Cindy was trying to get Freya to answer yet more. questions about what was going on.

Enrico took the phone back from her. 'You are now OK with this?' he enquired.

Only an idiot would try and ask him the same questions Cindy had been asking Freya. The call ended abruptly and, just like that, her son was being handed over to a stranger.

Power always at his elegant fingertips, she thought bitterly as the lift took them downwards. Her life had been taken over. Her son's life had been taken over. Hannard's and its entire workforce had been taken over.

She wished she could see even a tiny bit of difference between the three, but she couldn't. He was invincible, intractable…

More rotten adjectives.

She heaved out a sigh. The lift stopped. It took her a few seconds to realise that the doors were not opening, but it was only when she glanced at Enrico that she realised that he'd done it.

He'd stopped the lift between floors and was in the process of bending to place her box of things on the floor. He straightened up, and the stern cut of his expression was granite-like when he fixed his eyes on her.

'What?' she asked warily.

'You,' he answered.

'M-me?'

He closed the gap between them and Freya felt the sudden urge to start clawing at walls again to get away. She backed, one set of tense fingers making contact with cold metal, the other set clinging to his business case as if for dear life.

'This, then,' he said and lowered his mouth onto hers.

She should not have let it happen but it did. She hated him, so why did she let him kiss her like this? And he did kiss her, long and slow and so deep her head was swimming even before he leant his hips into hers. She felt the ridge of his arousal and her breathing feathered. His hand came to stroke the hand she had flattened to the lift wall.

It was such a sensuously tantalising gesture that deliberately mimicked an earlier one. He was playing games—sex games—using one of those Enrico Ranieri seduction techniques that could fell a woman without her really understanding how. Then he was moving against her rhythmically with that stroking hand. Luxurious desire just drowned her, heat pooling where he moved against her sending her legs weak.

Another demonstration of his power, she thought hazily. But it just wasn't fair that he could make her feel like this. It wasn't fair that every single inch of her was languorous and thick with need.

When Enrico drew away she couldn't move a muscle. If the lift wall hadn't been there she'd have fallen down. Her eyes were closed and her mouth was still parted, lips full and moist and pulsing—wanting more.

Bella, he thought. Irresistible. He did not know whether to be pleased by the evidence of how responsive she was to him, or be more convinced that she could not control herself around any man.

He hit the lift button to set it moving, then with grim silent precision tugged the elastic bands from her hair. The surprise sting to her scalp brought her eyes flickering open at the same moment as her hair tumbled down.

Eyes like dark green oceans stared up at him. 'There,' he said coolly. 'Now you look like the woman of Enrico Ranieri, all tousled and love-drugged and eager for me.'

It was the same as the slap of a hand across her cheek. In fact he could not have come up with a better way to pay her back for her earlier slapping of him. He could not have rendered her less able to react because her insides were still churning with pleasure, even if her brain was now functioning again.

He bent to pick up the box as the lift stopped again. Glancing down, Freya was stunned to discover that her fingers still curled around the handle of his business case.

Trained, she thought bleakly. Trained in so many ways three years ago to meet this man's needs that she'd stepped right back into her old role without knowing she was doing it.

The lift doors slid open on the ground-floor foyer. It was no longer lunch-time or a break-time, so the expanse of white marble was not as busy as it had been the last time she'd been here.

Still, there were enough people there to witness her exit from the building with Enrico's arm resting possessively along her slender back and his hand intimately curving the indentation of her waist.

Thoroughly kissed, dishevelled and now supported by a man who could not have made a better job of creating the impression he desired.

Freya kept her head down and refused to look at anyone. 'I...'

'Hate me, I know,' he finished for her. 'But say thanks to the fates for allowing you to wear those unflattering flat shoes today. If you had been wearing stilettos I would be carrying you out of here, you are so weak with desire for this man you hate.'

A black Mercedes saloon was parked at the kerbside. Enrico opened the rear door for her to precede him inside. Like a fully trained fool she went, moving across the seat so that he could get in beside her, simply assuming that they were to wait in the car until Fredo arrived with her son.

However, the car moved off almost as soon as Enrico had closed the door.

'But—w-what about Nicky…?'

'He will travel with Fredo,' Enrico answered.

'But you can't do that!' Freya straightened jerkily on the seat. 'How dare you do that?'

She was already twisting around to stare out of the rear window to look for the reassuring sight of another car keeping pace with them.

There wasn't one—not one of Enrico's kind, anyway.

It came to her then, the full, battering force of what was actually going on!

'You've stolen my son.' She turned hot, accusing eyes on Enrico. 'You've *stolen* him!'

He frowned. 'Don't be—'

'Stop the car,' she shook out, making a lurching dive for the passenger door, panic erupting like a spewing volcano as her hand closed over the lock. 'Stop this car so I can get out!'

On a thick curse Enrico was forced to stretch his long body out across the gap between them so he could clamp his hand over her hand to stop her from doing something crazy like diving out of a moving car.

'I have not stolen him!' he rasped out. 'Why would I want to steal my own son?'

'Where is he, then?' She fought him like crazy and she was shaking all over, body, voice. 'W-what have you done with him? How could you do this? How could you separate him from me? How can you be so utterly, totally thick and stupid as to—?'

'He is travelling by special taxi with Fredo because

this car is not equipped with a child safety seat yet!'
Enrico ground out, grimly restraining her by her wrists
while she continued to fight him to get free.

'Then I should be travelling with him, not with you!'

Her eyes flashed, her hair crackled and her body
heaved and twisted against him. His breath hissed from
his body as his frustration erupted.

'Stop this, Freya,' he muttered. 'You are hysterical.' It just had not occurred to him that she would
react like this to something that, to him, was merely
a practicality! 'You know that Fredo will take good
care of him!'

'That's not your decision to make!'

'It is now, *cara*, so get used to it.'

Angrily he threw her wrists aside and sat back in the
seat, leaving her to sit alone now that the first mad rush
of adrenalin was fading away—though the vibrations of
terror still raced through her. This latest demonstration
of his power over her showed that she was already
losing control of Nicky to him.

Stress sizzled up her backbone, the afternoon of
shocks and scares and battles culminating in a sudden
and blinding tension headache which held her there
stiff and tense on the seat. She closed her eyes and tried
to calm herself but she couldn't. She tried to swallow
over the dryness covering her throat but she couldn't
even manage to do that. Her heart was hammering away
against her breastbone, her breathing scored by fear.

Enrico watched her through narrowed glinting eyes.
She had turned as white as a sheet and her closed eyelids
were showing the fine bruising of strain. A streak of
angry remorse ripped through him. He had not meant

to scare her so badly when he'd had to hurriedly revise travelling arrangements on Fredo's advice. And it had actually suited him to keep the small boy out of the loop for now, while they were still fighting so many battles on every front.

He needed to keep the pressure on. If he relaxed it for a second she was going to walk away. Freya had to know as well as he did that he had no leg to stand on where Nicolo was concerned unless he travelled the long legal route through the courts to prove paternity.

At the moment, plain bullying was all he had going for him. Blunt tactics to keep her off balance and therefore easier to manipulate.

He wanted his son. In all his life he had never felt this powerfully overwhelmed by anything—unless he let his mind shift back three years to a moment he'd found this woman in bed with his cousin. For a moment he had been overwhelmed—with the desire to kill.

They left the London City perimeter and headed into Mayfair, accompanied by a silence inside the luxury car that stung and throbbed.

'Separating you from Nicolo was not a deliberate act of cruelty on my part,' he heard himself utter in a driven undertone and wondered why, after what he'd just told himself, he was now defending the deed.

'It's never happened before—never,' she whispered. 'He always goes everywhere with me.'

She turned her head to look at him, her eyes sparkling bright with vulnerable tears now.

Vulnerability got to him. His lips parted to offer an apology.

Then closed again. What a sucker, he mocked himself; so was his body, as that hungry animal called sexual desire leapt up inside to sink its burning sharp teeth into him and make him want to flatten her to the seat and remove that look by very physical means.

Hell, he was a bubbling collection of unfamiliar responses now. Did she think that she was the only one struggling to hold it together? This afternoon had been one long emotional roller-coaster ride since he'd stepped into Hannard's foyer.

And indulging in some hot, no-finesse sex in his office had not slowed down the ride any, he thought grimly. If anything, it had speeded it up and he'd been running on pure instinct ever since.

Hence the kiss in the lift, the lingering effects of which were still pumping around his system. Now the vulnerable look was feeding it, so was his bad temper and the sting of remorse, plus a thousand other not-so-easy-to-define feelings that were sending messages across the small gap separating them, and she let out a small, choked gasp.

She could feel it, too. Her breathing had quickened. Her colour was coming back, the vulnerable look slowly fading into something else.

The car made a right turn at a set of traffic lights. He lost contact with her eyes as she glanced outside.

'W-where are we going?' She began to stiffen.

Time to get tough again, Enrico recognised. 'My apartment,' he said. 'I decided it was best to start as we intend to go on, so your flat has been professionally packed up and should be delivered to my place by the time we arrive there.'

She blinked at him. 'But how did you get into my flat without—?'

'I took your keys from your bag while you were in the crèche.' Enrico pre-empted what was coming and allowed the next wave of shocks to echo between them. Then he went for the big one. 'Fredo is taking Nicolo to the zoo—to see the monkeys, I believe—so we can have a couple of hours before they arrive to get all the things Nicolo is familiar with unpacked and on show to help ease his confusion.'

He'd found another way to wipe out the vulnerable look, Enrico noted as he watched those green eyes change to chips of ice.

CHAPTER SIX

'QUITE the control-freak, aren't you?' Freya said coldly. 'I suppose you would love to make me disappear altogether. Then you could claim full control over Nicky!'

'Tempting proposition,' Enrico drawled lazily. 'I will give it some consideration.'

'And maybe I will do the disappearing without your help,' she flashed back.

'With no job and no money to aid you?' he mocked.

'I'm not totally without friends.'

Something stirred inside him. 'Men friends?' he demanded. 'Is there a man hiding in the shadows of your life who would be willing to finance this disappearance?'

'Maybe,' was all she said.

Something ugly changed the mood in the car. She'd taken him by surprise, Freya realised. It had not entered his arrogant head that there might actually be another man in her life!

'Who is he?' Enrico insisted angrily.

Triumph fizzed into life. 'I don't have to tell you that.'

The black eyes glinted. 'You do if you want to leave this car in one piece.'

'Get Fredo to bring me my son and I might tell you.'

'We are discussing *your* disappearance, not my son's. You can leave whenever you wish to. *My* son cannot.'

And that, Freya thought bitterly, said just about everything. 'Unless this man feels that he has prior claim on Nicky, of course…'

She was referring to Luca! Enrico knew that she was referring to Luca. Her heart began to palpitate as she held on to his gaze and watched him flick his eyes away from her, his handsome face turning to cold granite, each beautifully honed feature locking up tight.

The air in the car became too thick to breathe, some soft, weak instinct begging her to take the taunt back.

But he had stolen her son, Freya reminded herself.

Enrico could call it what he liked, but he'd separated the two of them to keep her compliant. That knowledge alone was enough to keep the retraction locked in her throat.

The car came to a timely halt then. Freya escaped by opening her door and climbing out, leaving Enrico sitting there—just sitting, with his cousin's name ringing inside his head.

A nerve punched in her tense spine as she stood taking in her surroundings. The afternoon was still hot and the sun was shining on the bright white walls of a Georgian property. This was not the same apartment block Enrico had used to live in three years ago; it looked a hell of a lot more palatial.

In fact, it didn't look like an apartment block at all, but more like a converted house. When Enrico arrived at her side to unlock the front door she wanted to ask questions, but the grim mood between them was conducive only to silence—a hard, tough, don't-look-at-one-another silence.

Inside, the wide, gracious hallway was the epitome of elegance, with a beautiful stairway leading up to the floor above. Freya had barely glanced around her before a door opened towards the back of the hall and a man appeared, dressed in tight jeans and a white T-shirt.

He pulled to a halt when he saw them. It was Sonny, Enrico's long-time housekeeper-cum-chef. Sonny was around the same age as Enrico and about as beautiful as a man could be. He was also as gay as they came and proud of it.

'Thought I heard you come in,' he said to Enrico, then flicked his gaze to Freya. '*Ciao,* sweetie; long time, no see,' he greeted. 'You have had one *bambino* since we last met, I hear…'

'Yes,' she answered—but did Sonny believe that Nicky was Enrico's son?

It had been Sonny's day off that time that Luca had come calling. Sonny only knew what he'd been told after the event. Enrico, Fredo and Sonny had grown up together on the huge Ranieri estate. Fredo and Sonny were Enrico's most trusted friends as well as his employees. If Sonny had heard Enrico's version, then Luca Ranieri's face was floating right here in the hallway between them like a cynical, mocking spectre.

As if he saw it, too, Enrico shifted tensely. 'Some coffee would be good,' he prompted Sonny.

'Sure.' Flicking his gaze back to Enrico, Sonny kept

his expression blank as he waved a hand towards a door. 'Freya's things arrived a few minutes ago. I was not sure what you wanted me to do with them, so I had them stashed in there…'

'OK, *gratzi*.'

The thanks doubled as a dismissal. After a final glance levelled at Freya, Sonny was nodding his dark head and disappearing back behind the door through which he'd appeared.

Enrico's hand arrived at the base of Freya's spine, making it stiffen in rejection. Ignoring her reaction, he applied pressure to make her move forward. The tension between them only helped to cleave her dry tongue to the roof of her mouth.

A few moments later and she was discovering that *in there* was a large drawing-room with French windows that opened onto a walled garden. The afternoon sun was streaming in through the glass, making the crystal chandelier that hung from the ceiling sparkle its rainbow patterns across the pale walls.

How the other half lived, Freya thought bleakly as she froze in the doorway to allow her gaze to drift over a designer's dream of a room, with its luxurious soft furnishings and spotless French-polished pieces of European antique furniture.

Enrico's old apartment had looked nothing like this. That had been luxurious, of course, but state-of-the-art modern and relatively easy for her to get used to, whereas this…

She tried to imagine letting loose a barely house-trained two-year-old in here and just couldn't. She was beginning to feel like a bag lady herself.

Enrico propelled her a few more steps forward, oblivious to his surroundings because he had always lived surrounded by the best. In fact, this room could have been picked up and transferred to here from his beautiful country estate outside Milan.

It was when he moved away from her to stride across the room that she saw the packing boxes stacked behind the door and froze yet again. For there stood her life, packed in what amounted to half a dozen boxes, plus a bright red-and-yellow child's rider-truck that looked so out of place she felt as if the room were glaring at it for daring to show itself.

'We can't live here,' she heard herself whisper.

In the process of pushing open the French windows, Enrico swung around then went perfectly still when he too saw the boxes and the red-and-yellow truck.

Something hit him hard in the mid-section of his body, insight into what Freya had been seeing when she'd whispered those words: her life packed into six damn boxes. Her small flat, the whole of which, he recalled, would fit into half of this room. She had no family left to call upon, no one but herself on whom to rely. Her cheap grey suit, scuffed shoes and hair that was in need of professional attention all seemed to make a mockery of the display of wealth that was on show here.

Then there was that brightly coloured truck; he could actually visualise his son sitting on it and careering across aged oak floors and priceless rugs, and knocking into finely tooled legs belonging to priceless tables and chairs.

Was the boy Luca's?

The question seeped like acid into his blood.

Was he in the process of making one of the biggest mistakes in his life?

Then—no, he thought, no.

'It is what I want.'

He said it oddly, as if the statement came to his lips directly from his suddenly aching gut. Maybe she heard it come from that deep place because she turned to look at him, green eyes big and so vulnerable he couldn't make his mind up whether to curse her for making his insides crease up the way they were doing, or to curse her for bringing Luca back into this.

'I have to go out…' The decision arrived out of nowhere. Enrico was already crossing back to the door when Freya's stare altered to one of surprise.

'But you said—'

'Get Sonny to show you around,' he interrupted brusquely. 'Choose some rooms to sleep in, unpack or—whatever. I will be back—later.'

The door shut behind him, leaving Freya standing there and wondering what had caused his sudden change of mind and his couldn't-escape-quick-enough exit.

Was he feeling their presence as an intrusion already? Had he looked across at her and seen the bag lady with the penchant for taking other men to her bed and wondered what the hell it was he was getting himself into?

Sonny appeared then, carrying a coffee tray and looking very wary.

'If you have something to say to me about this situation, then say it and get it over with,' Freya snapped at him. 'If not, then don't say anything at all and just—go away!'

With that she sat down in the nearest chair and burst into tears.

Sonny was good with tea and sympathy, though he probably thought privately she didn't deserve either, if he believed what he thought he knew about her and Luca.

And the tea was coffee...

But he mopped her up in his own unique, offhand manner. Made her drink some coffee, eat a small piece of his famously delicious home-made chocolate cake, then picked up one of her boxes and offered to show her around.

Enrico's place was huge, with the formal drawing-room she'd already seen, a dining-room and a very impressive book-lined study, plus a much less ostentatious but still glaringly elegant family-room and kitchen, all on the ground floor. Upstairs, the luxury didn't falter, she discovered. The master bedroom with its *en suite* bathroom was a work of art. Freya wanted to leave instantly—it was obvious that this was Enrico's room by the possessions she could see scattered around it, and she had no wish to linger there longer than she absolutely had to.

There were four further *en suite* bedrooms, one of which was already fitted out to accommodate a small child. When Freya quizzed Sonny about it, he reckoned that Enrico probably didn't know there was a child's room. In fact, Sonny was very forthcoming about how Enrico had bought the house—which apparently had a matching apartment on the two floors above them—unseen and fully furnished. He had moved in a week after he'd finished his relationship with Freya , and had spent only the odd night here since.

She chose the room next to Nicky's—it was the

furthest away from the master suite. Sonny had her boxes moved upstairs and Freya unpacked them with a deep-boned reluctance that showed in her taut expression and kept Sonny's tongue silent.

Nicky arrived two hours later, carried in Fredo's big arms. By the dark look on the bodyguard's face, he'd had more than enough of playing the nanny to an energetic small boy.

The moment Nicky saw Freya standing there in the hallway, he reached out to her with his arms and whimpered, 'Mummy!'

'Here, take him,' Fredo muttered. 'He's…tired.'

Tired didn't really cover it, Freya observed as she took hold of Nicky and let him curl up in her arms. He was dirty, a little smelly and definitely bad-tempered by the frown on his face.

'Had a good time, brown-eyes?' she asked him lightly.

'Fed the monkeys,' he mumbled. 'Daddy liked the tigers best.'

Daddy…? Freya lifted questioning eyes to Fredo, who responded with one of his shrugs.

'He came to find us after getting a child seat fitted in the car,' he told her. 'Then he dropped us off here before shooting back to Hannard's to put in a couple of hours' work.'

None of which explained how her son happened to be calling Enrico *Daddy*.

'You expected Nicky to call him Enrico?' Fredo challenged, reading her expression.

Freya honestly didn't know. The whole thing was moving so fast now she could no longer keep up. The tension headache was still thumping away at the backs of her eyes, and the *Daddy* seemed to make it all so frighteningly official.

'Want to go home now…' Nicky muttered.

And that, she thought heavily, started the next battle she had to wage before she could finally give in to misery and throw herself onto her chosen bed to indulge in a proper weep.

Did Enrico really think that he could just uproot them and plonk them down here and everything would carry on as normal? Did he think that turning up at the zoo and getting Nicky to call him *Daddy* automatically made him into a father?

'Let me show you what I've found upstairs first,' she suggested to Nicky with yet more lightness she just did not feel. 'Daddy has this *huge* house, with the biggest bath you've ever seen in your life!'

The little boy's curly dark head lifted off her shoulder. 'I want *my* bath,' he demanded sullenly.

'But you can swim in this one if you want to,' Freya said, winging a bright I'm-a-happy-mummy smile at her scowling son. 'And it makes frothy bubbles…'

Nicky didn't like his new bedroom. He didn't like the big bath. By the time—a couple of very long hours later—she had finally bathed, fed and lulled the over-tired, confused and fractious toddler into sleep in his new bed, it was all she could do to walk straight to her bedroom, strip off her clothes, take a quick shower then fall into her own bed.

Enrico stood leaning against the door-jamb, looking across at the flood of Freya's hair that streamed out across her pillows. She'd got into bed with wet hair, he saw, following the long trailing sections that looked heavy and darkened and damp. He could even smell the clean-scented shampoo from here.

He lifted a hand to rake his fingers through his own recently showered and shampooed hair.

He was tired and fed-up. Sonny wasn't talking to him: his housekeeper had taken exception to being left to deal with the new arrivals without much notice. Not his job, he'd said, to mop up after Enrico's women. It wasn't his job either to watch the mini-monster run rings around her while she was too tired and depressed to cope.

But now the mini-monster was sleeping the sleep of dark angels in a next-door bedroom.

His son. Enrico had gone to meet Fredo and Nicolo at the zoo this afternoon, and had spent time with the small boy, reaffirming that he was his father. When he was with Nicolo he knew it—knew it with every fibre of his being. It was only when the boy was not in his sights that the doubts crept back in.

Then he'd spent more time standing at his son's bedroom doorway, reassuring himself of it yet again as he watched Nicolo sleep.

Now here he was, standing here watching Freya and doing the same thing. A soft table lamp glowed beside her bed. A similar light was left on in the child's bedroom next door; the interconnecting door had been left ajar—presumably so Freya could hear if Nicolo awoke in a strange place and needed her.

He was on one hell of a steep learning curve here. The latest part of his ascent had been to learn that small children needed twenty-four-hour attention—to the extent that you tuned in even while you slept.

Which meant he could not close this door. A sigh eased from him. He made a mental note to employ a nanny as soon as possible, then stepped further into the room. Time to get tough again. Time to keep the pressure on, despite the exhausted sleep Freya had clearly sunk into.

Enrico crossed the room with the silent tread of bare feet on thick-pile carpet, carefully shrugged out of his bathrobe and laid it aside, then lifted up the duvet and eased himself carefully into the bed.

Freya stirred as the weight of his body disturbed the mattress. Reaching out for her, he drew her in.

'Enrico,' he heard her whisper. That was all.

At least it was *his* name.

'Shh.' He kissed her softly. 'Go back to sleep.'

To his surprise she did, sinking back down to where she had drifted up from, her cheek pillowed in his shoulder and her long legs unconsciously tangling with his.

Freya came awake to the sound of rattling crockery and the vague, stomach-sinking feeling that she had been abducted by aliens. She opened her eyes to find Sonny standing over her holding a breakfast tray.

'*Ciao,*' Sonny greeted. 'Orange juice, tea and toast for breakfast,' he listed, 'as instructed this morning by your much more amiable son.'

Nicky. A second stomach-sinking feeling hit her with a punch of reality. 'What time is it?' She sat up with a jerk. 'Where is Nicky?'

'The time is eight-thirty,' Sonny provided. 'And your son is, as we speak, on his way into the City with his papa and Fredo, affording you a well-deserved lie-in.'

The tray arrived across her lap, thereby effectively

trapping her to the bed before she could leap out and start yelling.

'Enrico said to tell you to eat, shower and calm down before you ring him at Hannard's.' Sonny pointed to a slip of paper lying on the tray. 'His private mobile number to cut out the middle man,' he explained drily. 'Oh—and I thought you would like to read this…' A newspaper arrived and was propped up against the teapot. 'Enjoy!'

Sonny strode out, closing the door very firmly behind him. Freya stared at her breakfast, then at the newspaper already neatly folded open at, presumably, the relevant page. Enrico had walked off with her son again. She'd slept in for the first time in over two years and had not heard anything, not even Nicky's good-humoured chatter, which had always, always been her early-morning alarm call and—

The print on the newspaper suddenly came into focus. With a sharp gasp she snatched it up and began to read. Thirty seconds later she was pushing the tray aside and diving out of the bed—it was only as she did so that she happened to notice the impression on the pillow next to hers.

Heat flooded into her, that stinging, stifling kind of heat which came with a half memory that could—should—have been the vague remnants of an old, familiar dream.

'Oh,' she choked and spun away to hunt down her handbag. Fishing out her mobile phone, she dived back onto the bed to pick up the slip of paper bearing Enrico's telephone number. Having been left to dry of its own accord, her hair was a mass of tumbling, twisting spirals that she had to push out of her way so she could read the digits and punch them out on the phone. Enrico answered immediately, though by then she didn't know which accusation to hit him with first.

'Y-you slept in my bed!' was the one that shot from her in a breathless shriek.

Enrico leant back in his chair and spun it round to smile at the view beyond his office window. '*Ciao, mi amore,*' he murmured dulcetly. 'You clung to me like a delightful but very possessive octopus, all arms and legs and—'

'That's a lie!' she gasped out.

'—made love to me as if I was your long-lost lover returned…'

'I did not! I would never—'

'…so wonderfully eager and so very insatiable…'

'You're just teasing me. Will you stop this—?'

'Had I not been so afraid that our son might sleep-walk into the room at any moment I would not have been able to resist. However…'

'I'm not listening!' she breathed down the phone at him.

'And miss out on the best part where I asked you who Nicolo's father is and you said—*You are*, Enrico…?'

Silence came at him across the airwaves. Glaring grim triumph now, Enrico waited for Freya to recover from the shock.

'I w-was asleep—'

'And so honest you even instructed me where and how I was to touch you.'

There was a sound like someone sucking in their breath. Were her eyes shut tight the way they had been last night? Was she standing or sitting or still lying there in the bed remembering her hot dream that had been so vividly real?

He got up, restless—angry now without knowing why, since he had managed to gain the upper hand over her in every way that he could. He could still taste her kisses on his tongue and feel her hands on his body, still feel her moving against him in that oh-so-sensuously pleading way and the warmth of her breath on his face as she'd whispered those soft, honest words to him: *He's your son, Enrico...*

'You begged me, *cara*,' he informed her brutally. 'You took hold of my hand and placed it where you wanted to feel it most. Then you came all over me in a sweet-scented, clinging rush and I—'

The phone went dead. Enrico was not that surprised that it had. He swung round to glare at his office, then swung back to look out of the window again.

Freya threw herself back on the pillows, eyes closed tightly, the racing thump of her heart locking up her chest so she couldn't breathe.

Her dream! The one she'd had so many times before. She'd thought she'd experienced it again so vividly last night. But it had been real!

She'd been somewhere between sleep and wakefulness. She remembered everything now: he'd come to her bed and drawn her against him, then kissed her softly on her mouth. *'Enrico.'* She could hear herself whispering. 'Shh,' he'd said. 'Go back to sleep.'

And she'd tried. She remembered sinking back down into the fluffy clouds of slumber where that dream always waited for her. But he'd moved then, tasted her mouth with the tip of his tongue and the rest had been—

Shameless; totally indefensible.

And, during their phone call, she hadn't even asked him about Nicky, which was even worse.

With a guilty groan she rolled off the bed and hit redial.

'You've stolen my son again,' she husked out.

'*Our* son is where he always is at this time of the morning—in my crèche with my very efficient care staff looking out for his well-being.'

Freya did not miss a single syllable of who was in possession of all the power.

'But I didn't even get to see him before you took him—'

'I didn't get to see him for two damn years,' Enrico said.

'So this is your idea of punishing me, is it? To separate the two of us and punish Nicky at the same time?'

'I am punishing no one.' His voice was heavy. 'I am merely attempting to make the best of a difficult situation for *all* of us—and don't cry, Freya,' he warned grimly when she tried to stifle her tears with a sniff. 'Weeping will only infuriate me in the present mood I am in. *Our* son is fine,' he assured her. 'He understood this morning when I explained that you were very tired so we were going to let you sleep. He came in to see you, gave you a kiss on your cheek. You smiled in your sleep, and he laughed because he seemed to recognise that smile in some special way. Then he was happy to let me wash and dress him—under his instruction,' he added drily. 'And for Sonny to feed him—with his supervision again. And for Fredo to deliver him to the crèche once we reached here.'

'I suppose it pleases you to make me redundant to his needs on all fronts,' she said.

'Except as a mother,' Enrico pointed out. 'For as long as he needs you as a mother, you will be there for him. For as long as he needs a father, so will I be. Get used to it, Freya. For this is how it is going to be from now on.'

'Hence the marriage announcement in the newspaper? *"Enrico Ranieri will marry Miss Freya Jenson, the mother of his two-year-old son, in three weeks—"'*

'Attempt to hide the truth and we risk turning it into a scandalous sensation,' Enrico cut in. 'We will present a united front on this,' he warned. 'For I will not have Nicolo subjected to taunts and mockery when he grows older because we tried to hide the truth.'

If you believed the truth to be Enrico's short statement explaining *exactly* how it had happened—and without Luca's name thrown in; he had so cleverly turned a twenty-four-hour disaster into the most romantic love lost, love found story.

'He's going to be very impressed when he's old enough to read it,' Freya muttered. 'But hear this, Enrico, because I mean it,' she then lashed angrily at him. 'You might succeed in possessing me as a wife, but you will *never* possess *me*, the person, again!'

Because her heart belonged to Luca? Enrico's fingers tightened around his telephone handset. 'And Nicolo need never know that his mother was a thieving, faithless love-cheat,' he responded coldly, 'so long as she never tries the same thing again, of course. Console yourself with that.'

Freya was to console herself with that bitter threat

many times over the next week, as Enrico demonstrated in every which way he could who was the one in complete control.

Like when she was sent out shopping with Sonny that same morning to refurbish her wardrobe, only to return and discover that Fredo had come back with Nicky at lunch-time—and a nice new nanny for her son.

Her name was Lissa and she was young, dark-haired and fluent in both English and Italian. Lissa, it turned out, had spent the whole morning with Nicky in the crèche so that by the time Freya saw them together they were like two very old friends.

When she discovered the bedroom she'd used the night before had been cleared of her stuff so that Lissa could use it and she was to sleep in the master suite—with the master, of course—Freya consoled herself by freezing Enrico out so totally that she actually shivered as she clung, wide awake, to the edge of the bed, and Enrico paid her back by not reaching for her once throughout the long, cold nights.

Each morning they played happy family across the breakfast table. Each morning Freya smiled nicely as she waved off Nicky, Enrico, Lissa and Fredo as they all trotted off to Hannard's without her, and only let the hurt ooze out when she was alone.

Nicky, it turned out, was to be weaned away from the Hannard's crèche and bonded with his new nanny in time for their move to Milan. Fredo always delivered him and Lissa back to Enrico's Mayfair house by lunch-time, when Freya was allowed to play the mother again.

And whatever else Enrico was trying to wean her son

away from, Freya could at least console herself with the knowledge that she was still the first person Nicky wanted when he was tired, hungry or upset because he'd hurt himself.

But how long would that last? How long before her importance to Nicky began to fade?

Each morning Sonny would appear with that day's list of instructions and off they would go to spend the morning transforming Freya into someone fit to be seen as the wife of Enrico Ranieri—and the mother of his son.

They became good fodder for the tabloids. The paparazzi followed wherever she and Sonny went. They called her a gorgeous and sexy redhead and they tossed questions at her about her past relationship with Enrico that she refused to respond to—until one dared to ask her if she'd been dumped three years ago in the same way that Enrico had dumped Sofia Romano last week?

Sonny was in the process of hustling Freya into a bridal shop when the question was posed.

'Who is she?' Freya demanded the moment they had privacy inside the shop. The fact that Sonny stiffened up was enough to make her freeze.

'Not my question to answer.' Sonny shrugged, and left it for her to find out the hard way—via the first newspaper she could lay her hands on.

Freya refused to try on any more clothes. She refused to be led around any longer by the nose. When another reporter dared to ask if Enrico was as amazing in bed as her predecessor had said he was, she answered kindly, 'Perhaps Miss Romano likes to exaggerate.'

They laughed, thought it hilarious. Sonny uttered an

under-the-breath groan. Freya sizzled quietly with anger all the way back to the house. The moment that Fredo delivered Lissa and Nicky, she took her son out again—sneaking out the back way and staying out with him all afternoon.

Enrico didn't laugh when he heard what she'd said. That night he showed her just how amazing he could be when he climbed into their bed and grimly hauled her across the gap.

CHAPTER SEVEN

'So, THE gorgeous and sexy redhead about to marry Enrico Ranieri has a sense of humour?'

Enrico was quoting directly from a newspaper article, his voice silken, the smile on his lips a circling shark's kind of smile.

Freya's pulse quickened. 'Miss Romano has a great sense of humour, too,' she hit back. 'She made me laugh all the way through my wedding-gown fitting after I read her account of how you fed diamonds around her slender wrist then murmured, "Sorry, but these mean farewell!"'

'What did you expect me to do—let her read about our marriage in the papers the next day?'

'Did the farewell and the diamonds come before or after our amazing sex?'

'You jealous, vindictive witch,' he gritted.

'And you are a two-timing rat!'

'I dumped her! How does that make me a two-timing rat?'

'You dumped her *after* you'd had *me* over your desk!' Freya lashed at him. 'That makes you the lowest kind of two-timer there is! Get *off* me!'

'I know a worse one.' Enrico clamped her flat against the silk-sheeted mattress with his impressively naked torso. '*She* two-timed two cousins in the same damn bed!'

'With your blessing, don't forget!'

'Don't start that again,' Enrico muttered.

'Then leave me alone,' she cried, pushing at him with her fists. 'I hate you. I don't know why I'm letting you do all of this to me. I don't even know how I've managed to share the same bed!'

'By clutching at the mattress to stop yourself rolling into me,' he derided. 'And I left you alone because I decided to at least attempt to give us both a proper wedding night—but to hell with that.'

In a single swift move he threw back the covers then came to straddle her, all naked rippling muscle and aroused, angry male. His hands went to the hem of her nightdress to tug it upwards; her fingers clutched at it to hold it in place.

'I won't let you,' she spat at him.

'You will be begging me in seconds.'

'I will not!'

He bent, becoming nothing more than a seething, dark, passionate blur as he lowered his head and took possession of her mouth.

No one ever said that making love had to be a gently-flowing river which slowly became a flood. Sometimes the raging torrent came first. As it did now, as tempers drove it and the desire to fight each other became as compelling as the desire to drown in each other's surging swell.

The kiss was their combat, a fight for supremacy

over her nightdress, a combat both knew he was eventually going to win. He was rock-hard and she took malicious pleasure in brushing against him with her knuckles and feeling him shudder and suck in his breath. He buried a set of fingers in her hair and tilted her head back so he could delve deeper into her mouth with the sensual stab of his tongue. She wriggled and squirmed and kissed him back, passion for passion. Their hearts were pounding, their breathing fast. When the thin silk slip was wrenched from her fingers, hot skin met with hers and she felt the flash of excitement sting in her blood.

'You ripped it!' she gasped as the silk was raked over her head and tossed aside.

'And you loved me doing it,' he rasped, before dipping his head lower to devour her pinprick, tingling breasts.

She cried out and scraped her nails down the skin of his back, sending tight muscles into rippling spasm. When he began moving lower she used her nails in his hair instead. The slide of his tongue was pure heaven. Goose-pimples sprang out across her flesh. She tried to arch her body up towards him but he held her flat to the bed, his hands cupping her hips and, with the force of his weight, he pressed her thighs apart.

His fingers stroked her either side of his lapping tongue. He explored her as no other man ever had. She was groaning—she could hear herself—groaning in sensual agony. 'Enrico,' she kept on saying as the muscles around her sex flowered and flexed.

He paused to look up, streaks of desire heating the golden skin across his cheekbones and glazing his darker-than-black eyes. She was almost there; he could feel the swelling, pulsing evidence of her climax balancing her right on the edge. Her hair was spread out across the pillows, cut and styled now to a thick and glossy spiralling pelt. Her eyes were shut, her arms thrown up above her head in wanton abandonment, her breasts shifting like two white mounds of female passion with their tight pink peaks urgently begging for his mouth.

Something hot washed right through him: desire for this woman like he'd never felt with anyone else.

'You want me,' he husked.

'Yes,' she whispered.

'Like this?' He licked across her clitoris.

Her whole body arched violently. 'No—!' she cried out.

'Like this, then!' In a single, snaking movement he arrived over her and with a thrust he probed her prepared flesh with the rounded tip of his shaft.

Her arms wrapped round him. 'Yes, like that.'

'You are begging me.'

She opened her eyes, bright green and sparkling with sensual accusation. 'Is this your ego joining in?'

'If you say so,' he responded. 'But I still want to hear you do it.'

'Do what?'

'*Beg,*' he rasped.

She captured his mouth in a deep, drugging kiss that was almost, almost the finish of his resistance. And she knew it, too; Enrico was sure she did because she timed it to the last, agonising split-second before she broke the kiss then begged softly: 'Please, Enrico.'

He sank his full length into her hot, wet sheath, then

tensed on a teeth-gritting groan as her muscles grabbed hold of him and clung.

'Dear God,' she shook out.

'*Madre de Dio,*' he muttered.

He moved and her legs wrapped tight around him. Bright sparks of pleasure hit the backs of his eyes. His skin was alive, fingers of pleasure clawing at every engorged muscle. He eased his hands beneath her hips and lifted her closer, recaptured her mouth, then began the long, deep, thrusting ride with the hard tips of her breasts rasping against his hair-roughened chest, and her fingers locked in his hair.

Time disappeared—space—the sweat-slicked, heaving stroke of their rhythm fusing them together into one pounding, pulsing sexual whole. It seemed to go on and on—the long pleasure before the short, blinding, white-hot pleasure, the glory of building towards the final climax that made the act of physical loving worthy of its name.

She broke first, on a whimper that tore their mouths apart. Her head went back, her fingers shifting from his hair to clutch at bunched muscles in his shoulders, and her small sobs grew louder as her pleasure quickened. Her pulsing muscles tugged and he joined her with long, thick, shuddering thrusts of his hips that left the two of them wasted.

He was lying heavy on top of her but he couldn't move a single muscle. She was lying so still beneath him he had a sudden image of her slowly melting into the bed.

It had only ever been like this with her—the lethargy that came with this kind of satiation that sapped every bit of his strength.

'Next time someone asks you how good a lover I am, what do you tell them?' he prompted on a low, lazy slur.

'Amazing,' she answered obediently. 'A real stallion.'

He grinned. A sudden spark of new-found energy gave him the strength to lever himself up on his forearms. 'That good, hmm?'

'A positive tomcat with a stallion's equipment,' she tossed up at him. 'A grand master in the art of sex. Would you like me to relay your performance to the Press?'

He laughed, even though he knew she'd not been joking. 'You,' he responded, 'are a jealous little cat with a very bad temper.' Then—'*Dio*, it's good to get the wedding night over with,' he sighed. 'Now we can have some fun instead of pretending we cannot stand to sleep with each other.'

He suddenly rolled away from her, then stood up and bent to scoop her up off the bed.

'What are you doing?' she protested.

'Continuing our premature wedding night.' Straddling her legs either side of his hips, he carried her towards the bathroom. 'You owe me for a week of sexual frustration, and one night in particular when you let me indulge you in totally selfish sex.'

'I was asleep,' she insisted primly, 'so it counts for nothing.'

'Oh, how very British,' he mocked. 'I was asleep, Your Honour, so I am therefore completely innocent.'

Freya couldn't resist it—she laughed. Enrico stilled in the bathroom doorway. Her slender arms were resting on his wide shoulders and her hair swung down her back. His eyes were steadily darkening as he took in the way the laughter highlighted every perfect feature in her beautiful face.

'You're so incredibly sexy when you laugh like that,' he growled sensuously.

Freya instantly changed the look for a scowl and he laughed, one of those deep-throated, husky sounds that vibrated pleasurably against her breasts.

'That look doesn't faze me—your eyes are still laughing.'

'So are yours,' she countered then kissed him on the mouth.

Freya didn't know which of them was more shocked. It had been purely an impulse reaction, one which came directly out of the few moments of relaxed banter they'd been indulging in. But it was the first time that she had taken the initiative and kissed him without being seduced into doing it.

Dangerous, she told herself even as she stared at him and he stared back, the tension between them tight. Don't let yourself fall back into the old love-trap you used to share with him once. Enrico is the enemy. He believes you can be like this with any man. It's your son he really wants. He's going to hurt you badly again if you don't watch out.

She went to pull away from him when his arms banded her closer. She sucked in her breath as her breasts crushed into his chest and with a throaty growl he recaptured her mouth. Dangerous or not she was right there with him, pleasure and excitement singing in her blood. Turning back the way they had come, he tumbled her back down on the bed then followed.

'I don't know how you do this to me but you do,' he muttered as he arrived on top of her, a seething-hot mass of satin-tight muscle and tensely aroused male.

His mouth arrived back on hers and her arms still clung to his neck. It took less than ten seconds for Freya to accept that she was lost, her common sense sunk without a trace in the dizzying knowledge that he couldn't help himself any more than she could.

They made love until the early hours and slept late the next morning while their son enjoyed running rings round his new nanny and Fredo.

The premature honeymoon to follow the premature wedding night, Freya likened a week later as she stood still while the designer Enrico had commissioned to make her wedding gown stepped back to view his creation along with Sonny, who went everywhere that she went, and Cindy, who was to be her bridesmaid.

They were discussing her but she didn't hear much of what they said.

She was too busy trying to work out how she had allowed herself to be so completely taken over by everyone—especially by the will of one very, very passionate man.

Was she being a fool for letting it happen?

Of course she was behaving like a fool, she admitted. Hostilities might have been halted for the time being, but the issues had not gone away and she needed to keep on reminding herself of that.

But it was just too easy to dismiss how this had all started out when everything else was going so right.

And Nicky was happy.

As the tension between her and Enrico had eased, the

whole household had relaxed and her son was flourishing in the new atmosphere. He was close to hero-worshipping Enrico. Fredo had become his very best friend. Sonny was his stomach's best friend and Lissa was like a big sister who was never too busy to play with him. The nanny was proving to be the ideal substitute to Hannard's crèche, which had played such a major part in the little boy's life. By the time they made the move to Milan in a few days Freya predicted that her son would barely notice the loss.

Even Cindy had said so. But then Cindy had bought into the whole love-lost-and-found fairy tale Enrico had carefully fed out there to the curious masses. She saw happy-ever-afters in everything Enrico said or did and made happen. He was even the romantic hero who'd invited Cindy to be Freya's bridesmaid when he discovered she had no one else to ask.

Freya'd lost touch with most of her college buddies four years ago when she'd moved in with Enrico and had begun to live a completely different life. When that relationship was over, she hadn't wanted to creep back to old friends with her tail between her legs, pregnant and miserable—and was too proud to let them know how badly she'd fallen flat on her face. After Nicky was born she just hadn't had time to develop new friendships.

Now, all of a sudden, Cindy was her best friend, and Cindy's new boss was the great guy who gave the crèche manager the week off work before the wedding took place. No bride could be more pampered and cosseted and indulged than Freya.

'She looks like a pagan princess,' she heard Sonny murmur.

I feel more like Cinderella, being given this one chance to know what it feels like to be a princess before the clock strikes twelve and it all vanishes.

Enrico sat contemplating the rings that had just been delivered to his office. Two matching gold wedding bands and a diamond eternity ring as was traditionally given on the birth of a first child.

Tradition was everything, he mused. He had gone all out to create a wedding for his son to remember and, although it was all taking place back to front, it was happening.

So why was he not feeling better about it? Why was he sitting here staring at these rings and feeling as if none of it was real?

Two weeks. In just two short weeks he had managed to pull off the most successful takeover he'd ever undertaken. He had his son living with him. He had the most sensually receptive women as a permanent fixture in his bed. In a few more days she would become his wife, then he would begin the legal process to claim Nicolo as his son.

It was all that he wanted—wasn't it?

No.

He wanted more. He wanted Freya to tell him out loud and unprompted to his face that Nicolo was his son. Other than for that one whispered confession she'd made while she'd been half asleep, she had not said it.

She had not come close to saying it.

She lived in his house and slept in his bed, she dived greedily and wantonly into his passion every night. She let him feed and clothe her and was even willing to let him marry her. He had made all the concessions, he thought arrogantly, so was this one small concession on her part too much to expect?

That night he made love to her as if it was going to be their last time. The next morning over breakfast he was bad-tempered and sour. When Lissa asked Freya if her bridal gown would be white or cream, her reply stoked his temper even more.

'I thought I gave explicit instructions that you were to wear a white dress,' he said tightly as soon as Lissa had disappeared to get Nicolo ready for his morning at Hannard's.

'I've got a two-year-old son born out of wedlock,' Freya mocked drily. 'A woman like me would have to be a real hypocrite to walk up the aisle wearing white. It's bad enough that you've insisted we have a church wedding!'

'I told you why I want that. I want there to be no blemish on our son's memory of the day his father married his mother. Our marriage will be as traditional as we can make it for him!'

For his son. It was always for Nicky.

'I don't see me causing him life-long damage by turning up to marry you in blue instead of white,' she snapped.

'The dress had better not be blue,' he warned very grimly.

Freya stuck up her chin to him and stared. 'It's my prerogative to choose what I wear to my own wedding.'

The look hit him right between the legs and he'd reacted to that ever-present sexual urge. 'While it is my money you're using to pay for every item you put on your back, you will wear what I tell you to!'

She went white. A hard silence hummed between them while she stared at him through pained green eyes. Her mobile telephone began to ring. Freya broke eye contact to pick it up and make the connection, hurt stinging the back of her throat.

'Hi, it's me,' a familiar voice said.

It was Cindy. They were supposed to be meeting up today in London to do some shopping, but Enrico's bad mood had put Freya in two minds as to whether to go. Then she remembered that she had something special she wanted to do, and got up from the table to turn her back on Enrico.

'Look, can't talk now,' she mumbled hurriedly. 'I'll call you back in a few minutes—OK?'

When she turned back to Enrico he was glowering. 'Who was that?' he demanded.

'None of your business,' she responded—then let out a yelp when he reached out and tugged her up against his chest.

'Tell me,' he gritted.

Freya pushed at him with the heels of her hands. 'My lover,' she taunted on angry impulse. 'The one who has a better temperament than yours and a hell of a lot more tact! We are planning to disappear together once I've used up your credit-card limit!'

His ensuing kiss was a hot, grinding punishment. By the time he released her she was pale and shocked.

'Don't play me for a fool, *cara*, or you will not like the consequences,' he bit out, then he grabbed up his business case and strode out of the room while Freya stared after him with a set of fingers pressed to her burning lips.

Her lips were still smarting when she called Cindy back to agree on a time and place for them to meet. In a fit of defiance she left the house without bothering to inform Sonny where she was going.

Her phone went while she was making her way to the nearest tube station. 'Where are you?' Sonny demanded.

'I've escaped,' she said caustically then broke the connection and in sheer defiance switched off her phone.

Enrico had a string of heavy meetings with Hannard executives all morning and was in no better frame of mind by the time he'd seen the last one out of his office and Fredo walked in.

One glance at his bodyguard's face and he sensed trouble.

'What?' he lanced out.

'It's Freya,' Fredo said, then he shifted his weight from one foot to the other in a very uncharacteristic show of uncertainty and Enrico felt a warning sting attack the back of his neck.

'What about Freya?'

'No one has seen her since this morning after you left the house.'

'She will be out swapping her blue wedding gown for a white one,' Enrico said grimly, picking on the point of conflict that had flared between him and Freya this morning as a way of dealing with this worrying information.

But Fredo gave a shake of his head. 'Sonny says that the dress was never blue in the first place. She was just teasing you.'

Making him rise to the bait, Enrico thought and sighed, aware that his bad temper this morning had deserved to be hooked.

'Then where did she go? Didn't Sonny—?'

'Sonny said she made a call on her mobile just after you left, and the next thing he knew she'd gone out.'

A phone call. It was crazy to let it happen, but that hit him right in the centre of his chest. He shifted his stance impatiently, wishing he could trust her, but knowing only a mad, love-blind fool would do that.

'How long ago?' he demanded.

'Four hours,' Fredo supplied. 'And that's not all...'

There was more...? Enrico glared at him.

'She disappeared for several hours last week, too, only she had the *bambino* with her that time. *He* said they'd been to the park to feed the ducks but...'

'But—what?' Enrico incised, not liking the expression he could see on Fredo's face.

'We could not locate Luca...'

'I know that.' Enrico frowned impatiently. 'I've got people tracking him down.'

Luca was another problem he still had to deal with. His cousin was out there somewhere but none of the people Enrico had looking for him could find him. All they knew was that he had left his rich mistress in Hawaii, caught a flight to New York then just disappeared.

'They have tracked him,' Fredo said, grabbing Enrico's full attention. 'One of the investigators received word of his whereabouts last night but only got around to reporting it to me five minutes ago.' Fredo paused for a second then heaved in a deep breath. 'You are not going to like this, Enrico,' he warned grimly, 'but Luca has been here in London since last week…'

That sting at the back of Enrico's neck became a full throb. His mind's eye pushed an image in front of him of Freya standing there, dressed in a sassy grey suit and glaring at him as she taunted him with another man.

Luca? Had she been taunting him with the truth?

Then—no, he told himself. He was not going to let his mind go down that route.

'Where is Luca staying?' he asked tightly.

'He's crazy enough to be using one of your hotels.'

Of course it had to be one of his hotels, Enrico thought grimly. Luca had always coveted his cousin's possessions—his wealth, his standing in the family, his hotel accommodation, his woman…

It came without warning, but he found himself reliving a flashback to three years ago when he had caught his cousin and his lover lying in a twisted clinch of limbs on his bed. He could see the discarded heap of male clothes on the floor and the way her robe had been flung open wide on either side of her as if they'd been too eager to bother taking it off. They were heaving and panting, rushed and desperate, her hair flying all over the place, her fingers gripping Luca's head as she'd kissed him with that all-consuming—

Damn, he cursed, and switched off the image. Stop going there! he told himself.

'The guy tracking him hung around the hotel to do some sleuthing,' Fredo was saying. 'A woman arrived there this morning. He followed her up to Luca's suite…'

There was another pause—one of those long, uncomfortable pauses that made Enrico flick Fredo a hard, warning glance. The bodyguard grimaced, clearly unhappy about what he had to relay next.

'She was a long-haired redhead, Enrico,' he announced heavily. 'A tall, slender redhead wearing a grey suit…'

Freya arrived back at the house feeling as if she'd done the London marathon. Her feet were aching through trailing in and out of just about every store the city had to offer with the disgustingly energetic Cindy, who'd been determined to fill every precious second of her time off from Hannard's.

Oh, what a sad soul you've turned into that you can't even stay the course of some girly shopping, she mocked herself wearily as she climbed up the stairs carrying bags stuffed within bags, trophies of the spending spree she'd indulged in, using Enrico's credit cards in outright rebellion after his nasty comment about her spending his money.

Only one item in the bags had been bought with her own money. And that one small item had been cheap by Enrico Ranieri's exalted standards, yet it had still depleted her tiny savings to an alarming degree.

She was going to have to do something about that, she thought frowningly as she stepped into the bedroom. As soon as this marriage thing was out of the way and they'd settled in Milan, she would have to go job-hunting and grab back her independence from this—

'Where have you been?'

In the process of dumping her bags on the floor, Freya looked up in surprise to find Enrico standing in front of the window, his hands stuffed into his trouser pockets and his jacket flipped back to reveal his bright white shirt, which was delineated by the dark silk strip of his slender tie. He looked long and lean and totally sexy.

Her senses lit up. She really should be doing something about smothering them, she told herself, because the man was still and always would be the circling shark she couldn't trust.

'Out,' she answered, not seeing any reason why she should offer up more than that, when it was obvious what was stashed in the store bags. 'Why are you back here so early?'

'It is four o'clock—'

'Seven is closer to your rolling-in time.'

'And you have been out for most of the day.' He ignored her sardonic response.

'Don't my feet know it!' Dropping the last of the bags, she sat down on the end of the bed and with a sigh kicked off her shoes.

Her hair shimmied forward as she bent to rub at her aching toes and the throbbing balls of her feet.

The silence from the window stretched like tension wire and eventually forced her to tilt a look at him. He hadn't moved. He didn't appear as if he was even breathing.

Was he still miffed about the blue wedding dress…?

Well, she wasn't going to tell him the truth. He could wait to find that out the *traditional* way when she walked down the aisle. She was the bride who knew she should not be allowing herself to be a bride, even though she was doing nothing to stop it from happening.

Because you're weak, she chided herself. Because,

despite everything he did to you three years ago, you're still such a fool where he is concerned that you just can't bring yourself to call a halt to it.

'Something wrong?' she asked innocently, refusing to let him know that the morning's row was still pulsing through her bones.

He didn't answer, and his dark silhouette, backlit by the sun coming in from behind him, began to take on the shape of a grim reaper. Looking away again, she frowned as she continued to rub at her feet. She knew that Nicky was fine because she'd just met him and Lissa on their way to the park as she'd walked back from the tube. They were going to play football. Her son wanted an ice cream from the park café, so she'd handed over some coins and managed to steal a quick hug before he'd raced off with Lissa in charge of his hand.

Any other time and she would have been begging to go with them, but after a hard day's shopping her feet just—

A sudden gasp broke from her as the pair of black leather shoes that appeared in front of her took her by surprise; she had not heard Enrico move.

She looked at the same moment that he bent to grasp her elbows. The next thing she knew she was being propelled to her feet by hands that were not gentle.

'What the—?' she began, but his mouth took the rest away, crushing her lips with a hard, bruising kiss that completely stole her breath.

She tasted of Freya and she smelled of Freya and she kissed him back like Freya always did whether she wanted to kiss him or not! Enrico thought angrily. And he wished he knew why the hell he was kissing her at all, when what he should be doing was throwing her out of his life the way he had done the last time that she'd done this to him.

Had she kissed Luca like this today? Had she enjoyed playing one cousin off against the other again? Had she paraded her son in front of Luca to hedge her bets in case Enrico did not come through with what she wanted from him?

Or did she really not know which one of them was Nicky's father?

Well, he could tell her. He *knew* the answer without asking the question!

He pushed her from him, cursing the way his body was burning for more of her while the deep pit of his anger gushed like iced water through his blood.

'What was that for?' she choked, shoving a set of fingers up to cover her ravished lips.

'I have to go away.' He turned his back on her, stiff-shouldered, stiff-damn-everything! 'I will not see you again until we meet at the church.'

'So that was meant as a farewell kiss, was it?'

She sounded shaken and shocked and he wanted to swing round and strangle her—but he had his son to consider, and a marriage to get through to secure Nicolo's place in his life.

'Sorry to tell you this, Enrico, but your technique is slipping.'

'Put it down to pre-wedding nerves,' he heard himself respond with only a slight hint of sourness.

'Just say the word and we can call it off.'

The offer pulled him up short just as he was about to

leave. He really thought he could live this lie through until she was safely married to him—but he found he could not.

His control exploded and he turned on her, his expression savaged by anger and contempt. 'I know about Luca!' he ripped out harshly.

She stopped rubbing her bruised lips to look up at him. 'You know what about Luca?' she asked.

So wide-eyed and innocent, he thought cynically. And the hair—the damned hair! Loose and flowing and shining like silk around her perfect face!

The bitch, the *bitch*—he had to clench his fists together to stop himself from reaching for her long, white, satin-smooth throat. He wanted to hate her so badly that the need burned like acid in his blood.

But he did not hate her, he—

'You met with him today in London,' he enunciated over the hard rock of other words blocking his throat.

'I did not!' she denied.

'And on at least one other occasion in the last two weeks.'

Freya was looking at him now as if he had gone mad. 'I haven't set eyes on your awful cousin since you kicked him out of your apartment three years ago, and nor do I ever want to,' she insisted. 'Where did you get the crazy idea that I have?'

'I had him tracked down to a hotel close to here—'

'Good for you.' She mocked that. 'What has it got to do with me?'

He made a tense, tight movement with his body that seemed to help him to pull in air through flaring nostrils.

'A woman was seen going into his suite,' he informed her. 'She was a redhead.'

Freya stared at him open-mouthed. 'And you're assuming that the redhead was *me*?'

'Don't look so innocent,' he disparaged. 'It may not have been my own eyes that witnessed your betrayal this time, but the description said it all!'

CHAPTER EIGHT

ENRICO swung away from Freya as if he could not stand to look at her.

'Wait a minute…' She stepped up to grab his jacket sleeve and pulled him back around. Her legs were shaking, her insides beginning to succumb to nausea. 'Are you telling me—' she tried to keep her voice calm but was not successful '—that you believe I met with your cousin behind your back only two days before I am due to marry you?'

'Twice, that I know of.' He pulled his sleeve free as if her touch offended.

Hell really does freeze over, Freya thought coldly as she felt it happen right there and then.

'That's a lie,' she breathed out icily.

'Don't play that one again,' Enrico denounced. 'I have heard it before and I am no sucker for it. You met with him today.'

Freya didn't answer.

His eyes flashed black murder. 'You even took *my son* with you on the first occasion when you met with him last week!'

Folding her arms beneath her breasts, she faced him out. 'You know that for a fact, do you?'

'The evidence stacks up.'

'It can only be circumstantial evidence,' she declared. 'But then you have always enjoyed thinking the very worst about me!'

'Do you believe I *enjoy* being reacquainted with the real person behind the pretty face and honest green eyes?' he demanded.

'Don't forget the I'll-take-it-since-it's-on-offer hot sex!' she lashed back.

'You are as turned on by the sex as I am,' he derided.

Her chin went up. 'You mean, like a cheap tramp?'

He frowned. 'I did not say that.'

'But you think it, Enrico, or you would not be saying these things to me at all!'

He turned his back on her again. 'You should have stayed away from him.'

'Oh, I don't know!' Shaking badly now, she turned to walk back to the bed then bent to rummage in her shopping bags. 'Luca is beginning to come out of this the better cousin all round. At least he *knows* he's a piece of low-life! Whereas you dare to kid yourself you have a right to take the moral high ground!'

Straightening up, she threw something at him. It landed with a hard clunk against his back then dropped to the floor at the heels of his shoes. Enrico turned, frowning as he looked down and saw a flat gold-wrapped package tied up with a cream satin ribbon.

'Open it,' she instructed. 'See for yourself what I was really doing while you believed I was screwing your cousin in a hotel room!'

The fine hairs at the back of his neck were on the rampage again as Enrico bent to pick up the package. The sound of broken glass crunched beneath his fingers—fingers that were not quite steady as he undid the ribbon and unfolded the paper to see what was contained inside.

Freya was trembling from head to foot as she watched him do it. Never in her life had she felt so angry or hurt by him. Suddenly Enrico went perfectly still, his eyelids hooded so she couldn't gauge the expression in his eyes and her own blurred with hot, wounded tears.

'I had to wait for two hours while the registrar reproduced that exact copy of Nicky's birth certificate,' she informed him unsteadily. 'Then I spent another couple of hours trawling London looking for just the right frame to mount it in.'

The glass was broken now, split into several sharp-edged shards, but the gold-edged and mirrored frame was still intact, complete with its hand-etched inscription.

Thank you, it said, *for our beautiful son.*

'You named me as his father.' The statement arrived from Enrico flat and low.

'Yes!' Freya tried to laugh but didn't quite make it. 'Childish of me, I know, to keep on denying it when it's been right there all the time in black and white, but you…' She stopped to pull in a breath. 'When I decided that you deserved to know the truth I came up with this…silly gesture. It was meant as my wedding gift to you but…'

'It is not silly.'

'W-whatever,' she dismissed. 'As you see, you don't

really need to marry me to secure a place for yourself in our son's life. You've always had it. I was going to give you that on our wedding night as a…'

Token to show my commitment to our marriage. But she couldn't say it, not now, because it was no longer relevant. There was not going to be a marriage.

'Who called you this morning before you went out to do this?'

He *had* to ask that, didn't he? He just couldn't let the Luca thing go! And he hadn't looked at her once since he'd bent to pick up the gift. Was that because he was too busy kicking himself for not bothering to check out Nicky's birth certificate *before* now? If he had done, he would not be stuck in this bedroom with a woman he could not trust as far as he could spit!

'Cindy,' she answered, her voice hardening now as the tears turned cold and her chest closed up. 'We'd arranged to spend the day together doing…' What any bride and her bridesmaid would do before the wedding, shopping for frivolous things like the sexy underwear and the sheer nightdress that lay in one of the shopping bags and… 'So if you require a witness to confirm how I spent my escape time—refer to her.'

Enrico moved then, jerkily. He lifted his head to look at Freya, only to find that she had already turned away. His throat was working, his eyes felt sunken into his head beneath a remorse that was tearing his insides to shreds.

'I'm—sorry,' he uttered inadequately.

Freya just shook her head. His apology was too little and too late for her to want to accept it.

She heaved in another thick breath. 'I've tried to see

everything from your point of view. I even understood why you believe what you do about me.' It had been damning evidence, after all—first-hand evidence. 'I h-hoped that this time we could make a go of it and put the past behind us for Nicky's sake, if not for our own. But this thing with Luca has shown me that it's useless. You will always despise and resent and suspect me of being a cheap little tramp who trips from cousin to cousin without a single twinge of guilt.'

'I don't see you like that.'

'You do see me like that,' she rounded on him. 'And you know what, Enrico? I *feel* like the tramp who sold herself cheap to you!'

'You had a thing going with my own damn cousin!' He went on the attack again.

'I had a stronger thing going with you until you well and truly put it to death,' she threw back.

'You expect me to ignore what you did three years ago?'

'Three years ago I was lied about, falsely accused and given no chance to answer the charges. I was insulted and humiliated, then thrown out of your life! Do you remember how I begged you to believe me, Enrico, how I told you I was pregnant with your baby, wept all over you? Do you recall how disgusted you were that I dared to put on such an unseemly display in front of your oh-so-righteous self? And how you removed me from your person like I was something a passing bird had dared to drop on you, then had me escorted—*escorted*,' she shrilled at him, 'from your presence by the ever-faithful Fredo, who had to witness my final indignity when I threw up in the nearest loo?'

Enrico had grown paler by the second, and so he should do, Freya thought bitterly, taking his discomfort as her due.

'I wasn't even allowed time to pack my own things,' she continued thickly. 'They were *sent* to me in a cardboard box marked "Personal Effects of Freya Jenson" as if I were a dead woman.'

Eyes stinging, mouth wobbling, Freya had to turn her back on him again and so missed the way he stiffened in shock.

'I did not organise the return of your belongings.' His voice came to her like a dark cloak being thrown over her.

'Well, that absolves you, of course. Good for you.'

'*Per Dio,*' he rasped. 'I was upset! You cannot begin to imagine how I was feeling at that time!'

'Fooled, wounded, betrayed?' she twisted round to lance at him.

'*Si—si–si!*' He threw out his hands. 'Deeply fooled, deeply wounded, *deeply* betrayed!'

'Well, hey!' Freya cried, throwing open her own arms in a matching gesture. 'Look at me, Enrico, standing here feeling all of those rotten things, too! And you want me to feel sorry for you?'

He made a move like a man at war with himself now. 'I still see it,' he admitted harshly. 'Each time I let myself think about Luca, I see what you were doing with him!'

'And I still see the man I loved standing there condemning me instead of trying to defend me,' Freya shook out, 'which kind of says it all about what we were intending to do here.'

'What is that supposed to mean?' His head came up, eyes like black diamonds glittering inside the pale mask of his face.

She wanted to hate him. Oh, how badly Freya needed to hate him! But she loved him! And that was the most tragic part of all of this.

For an answer she turned and walked into the dressing-room. There was a twisted kind of irony in the way she bent to pick up a cardboard box still half unpacked and carried it into the bedroom. She placed it on the bed, then started opening drawers to toss things into it.

'What the hell do you think you are doing?' Enrico lanced at her.

'Packing,' she answered. 'Getting out of your life.'

Only this time she would do her packing herself.

He strode across the room and wrenched her round to face him. He looked as pale as death. 'You believe that I will let you do this? You believe I am going to let you walk away with my son?'

His son—*his* son. It had always only been about Nicky. She'd only ever been a means to an end, with a bit of good sex thrown in! All his nasty thoughts about her and Luca he had so carefully stored up to keep him in touch with his reasons for marrying the likes of her at all!

Where had her brain been? Lost in the clouds, she answered her own stupid question. Living out a three-year-old dream, when everyone knew that dreams didn't come true!

'I will not let you do it to *him*.'

Ah, the big one. The one and only reason fit to make her stop and think. Nicky adored this man. He loved his

newly extended family. Could she rip him away from
all of this…?

'If I can overcome what I witnessed three years ago
and marry you for our son's sake, then you can
overcome that today I seem to have made a mistake
about you and Luca.'

Hedging his bets, Freya noted bleakly. She just knew
he was going to check her story out before he really let
himself believe a single word that she'd said.

His fingers bit into her arms when she said nothing,
her eyes glassed over like ice. 'Are you listening to
me?' he demanded roughly. 'Nicolo deserves that you
do this. He has a right to the life I can offer him and
which you cannot!'

And that, Freya thought, was the real bottom line.
Enrico had everything with which to give Nicky the
life that he deserved, and she could not take that away
from her son.

She took a step back from him, swiping his fingers
away as if they made her skin creep. 'I want you out of
this bedroom,' she quivered out. 'I don't want you to
touch me ever again.'

'That's just—'

'The way it is going to be from now on, Enrico,' she
cut over him. 'Because I will *not* pay the price any
more for what your rotten cousin did to me. And I will
not be the victim of your lack of trust. You wanted a
marriage of convenience for Nicky's sake? You've got
one—on my terms. So now, get out.' With that she
turned and walked into the bathroom and slammed the
door shut.

Sizzling with helpless rage, Enrico turned and

stormed out the bedroom door, wondering how he had got it so wrong.

Fredo was waiting downstairs in the hallway.

'Get your informant on the bloody phone!' Enrico raked at his bodyguard on the way to his study.

Fredo already had his mobile to his ear as he followed his boss. Two minutes later, digital photographic evidence of the redhead caught on camera as she entered Luca's hotel suite flashed up on Enrico's computer screen.

Silence followed while both men stared at the image. Then the bodyguard released a soft curse that just about covered the way Enrico was feeling. 'It's not her,' Fredo muttered.

He also sounded relieved.

Enrico wasn't relieved; if anything he was all the more angry. He had just made a complete idiot of himself and totally alienated Freya at the same time! Two weeks of careful planning had just been tossed out of the window.

Now what did he have?

He looked down at the broken frame resting on the desk in front of him. His eyes burned in his head as he reread the details of his son's birth then the message inscribed on the frame.

She had done this for him. She had thought it through and prepared this wedding gift because finally she had been ready to trust him.

In doing so she had given him everything he'd believed he wanted, but now it felt as if he had just lost everything.

I still see the man I loved standing there condemning me instead of defending me.

Por Dio, could she have been telling him the truth?

He saw it all again, that tormenting flashback to Freya and Luca lying in a twisted clinch of limbs on his bed with her slender white fingers gripping his head.

She had not been holding him to her in throes of passion; she had been tugging viciously at his hair! And she had not been kissing him hungrily; she had been desperately trying to bite!

'Leave me,' Enrico rasped at Fredo without lifting his head up.

'Enrico, you—'

'Just go.' He interrupted whatever Fredo's anxious voice was going to say next.

Enrico needed to be alone. The details he had never allowed himself to look at before were coming to him fast now: the whitened look of shock on her face that had changed to relief when she'd seen him standing there; the way she'd hit Luca hard enough to send him rolling off her; the dizzy manner in which she'd scrambled off the bed. 'Enrico—thank God,' she'd sobbed out at him.

The door closed behind the retreating Fredo. Tears were stinging at Enrico's eyes and his throat. He was seeing the bruised swelling that had been on her bottom lip now and the finger marks on the creamy globes of her breasts as she'd dragged her robe around her to cover herself up.

He was also seeing himself standing there frozen and unyielding as she'd stumbled towards him.

'*Por Dio*,' he repeated hoarsely, then dropped into the chair and covered his face with his hands.

Upstairs, Freya was standing in the bedroom, still

shaking in the aftermath of the ugly scene with Enrico, when her mobile phone began to ring. Unearthing it from the depths of her bag, she then just stood there staring at it while it jangled in her hand.

Its caller-display was telling her it was Cindy. She did not want to speak to anyone right now but she couldn't ignore her bridesmaid.

With a flick of a button she made the connection. 'Hi, Cindy,' she said as casually as she could.

'So, *cara*, you have a son,' a deep, smooth-as-silk voice murmured pleasantly. 'I congratulate you on convincing my cousin that the child is his—or is he convinced? Maybe I should check this *bambino* out for myself.'

Freya tossed the phone away as if it had bitten her, her feet backing her away from it as she watched it land on the floor by the bed. Her eyes had turned black with staring horror, a line of white tension circling her trembling mouth.

It wasn't! It couldn't be. It was as if she'd conjured him up out of the morass of ugliness she'd just been through with Enrico. Though it was Cindy's phone number on the display, she had heard Luca's voice! How could it be *his*?

Luca, she repeated. Dear heaven. Her stomach turned over as the truth really hit. Luca had somehow got his hands on Cindy's mobile phone and was using it to call her!

A sound outside the bedroom window told her that Nicky and Lissa were back from the park and playing in the walled garden. Her mobile began to ring again, flipping her attention from one familiar sound to the other. Her shaken brain took seconds to realise that the way she'd tossed the phone away must have severed the original connection.

That was the moment it really sank in, what Luca had said, and she dived down to snatch the phone up.

'Y-you stay away from my son!' she bit out shrilly.

'And miss this opportunity to pluck my cousin's god-like wings?' Luca mocked. 'How much do you think the tabloids will pay for my kiss-and-tell exposé, *cara*? I can see the headline: *Tycoon's Sex Shame! Cousin tells all about bed-swapping with Enrico Ranieri's bride!* What do you think—it would be a nice wedding present?'

'It's a lie!' Freya breathed.

'Where in what I can describe is the lie?' he challenged. 'Were we or were we not discovered together in Enrico's bed?'

Freya was so icy cold now she was shivering, the sickness clawing at the walls of her throat. In some other part of her brain she was aware of Nicky's laughter drifting up from the garden, and the addition of Enrico's voice as he spoke to his son.

His son!

Drawn by something she could not put a name to, Freya moved on shaking limbs to the window and looked down in time to watch Nicky run to his father, who was squatting down with his arms held open to receive the little boy.

Tears blurred the image out. 'W-why don't you crawl back into your dark hole again, Luca?' she said thickly. 'No one wants to listen to your lies here.'

'Enrico will listen—as he did the last time. All of

Europe will listen when I tell how he threw both of us out three years ago after he caught us together in his bed.'

'He will kill you before he will let you do something so vile.'

'He would need to find me first,' Luca laughed. 'Mud sticks, *cara*, and I will be long gone before this particular mud hits its target, with my fat payment from the lucky tabloid safely stashed inside my wallet.'

'So why are you bothering to warn me about it?'

'To make you sweat?' he suggested. 'Or to give you the opportunity to make me a better offer for my silence.'

'I don't have any money.'

'I know. Such a poor little rich wife you are going to be, are you not, Freya? With Enrico keeping you short on cash because he cannot trust you with it and also having you watched night and day in case you decide to tumble into bed with other men.'

'Get to the point of this call, or I will cut the connection!' she sliced out.

'You won't do that. You are too damn scared.'

He was right: she was scared—terrified of the damage Luca could do to that small boy she could see down there riding on his father's arm with a look of total adoration on his face. The late-afternoon sun was catching Enrico's lean, dark profile. Freya's heart turned over then gave a tight squeeze, because she could see even from up here the grim austerity underlining the warm smile Enrico wore for their son.

She was going to have to tell Enrico, she realised bleakly. She just dared not risk giving Luca the chance to carry through his threat and sell his story to the Press.

Her mind reeling, she walked across the bedroom, her face turned ashen now, because she knew what she was going to have to do next.

'H-how did you get hold of Cindy's mobile?' she asked huskily as she quietly pulled open the bedroom door.

'I—borrowed it,' Luca answered drily. 'Or a friend of mine did.' For some reason he found that last remark funny enough to make himself laugh. 'I would imagine your bridesmaid is hunting through her many bags of shopping looking for it, as you and I speak.'

'Stealing from others again, Luca?'

Her insides were a twisting, quivering mess and her legs felt as if they'd been attached to live cables that made them tremble, as she walked down the stairs still clutching her phone.

'It was necessary for me to reach you without going through Fredo or Sonny,' Luca drawled.

'Or worse—through Enrico,' Freya put in as she crossed the hall and entered the drawing-room, where the crystal chandelier reflected rainbows across the pale gold walls. 'You accuse me of being scared, Luca. But I know you're scared of Enrico, or you would be having this conversation with him not with me.'

Silence met that last statement. The kind of silence that told her she had hit a raw nerve. Freya took grim pleasure in knowing it as she crossed the drawing-room floor.

'I would watch what you say to me, *cara*,' Luca came back eventually. His pleasant tone had disappeared now and a grimly threatening growl had arrived in its place. 'I am the one in a position of power here. I can ruin your romantic wedding day with one easy phone call.'

Freya stepped through the open French windows into soft sunlight, its warm gold colour shimmering across her hair and her cold, pale skin. Nicky was riding his truck, skidding down garden pathways and showing off for Enrico.

Enrico must have heard her footsteps, because he spun round sharply. Freya's breath caught in her chest, imprisoned there as she mentally compared the hard, handsome qualities that this Ranieri man before her possessed to the weak good looks of the one she was listening to on the phone.

They were really nothing like each other, she realised with an inner start of surprise. They might possess the same basic Ranieri features. But it was the way in which those features were arranged that made this man in front of her such a visibly dynamic force to look at, while the other was just a paler version—like a shadow without any substance.

Enrico took a step towards her, his lips parting as if to speak.

Freya stopped him with a quick warning shake of her head. 'If you're going to use blackmail, Luca,' she said as coolly as she could in the circumstances, watching as the sound of his cousin's name made Enrico stiffen fiercely, his face darkening into a savage black, questioning frown, 'then why don't you just get to the point and tell me exactly what will stop you talking to the Press?'

Without a pause, she handed the phone to Enrico, then just stood there, heart hammering as he put the handset to his ear.

'I want you to jilt him at the altar,' Enrico heard Luca

say smoothly. 'Nothing short of his public humiliation will do for me, *cara*. I want him to know how it feels to be cast aside like he is nothing. I want him to learn that, even with all his wealth and power and popularity, when it comes down to it his pride can still be wiped away under someone else's feet. Are you listening to me, Freya…?' he prompted suddenly, maybe aware that her silence was different.

Without saying a word, Enrico placed the mobile phone to Freya's ear and gave a curt nod of his head.

'Y-yes,' she answered obediently.

The handset was removed again. Enrico listened without expression as Luca finished his blackmail pitch.

'Do this for me and I will hold my silence with the newspapers,' he promised. 'I will even let your son keep his papa. God knows I have no desire to claim the boy and we both know it would be a battle I could never win with medical science being what it is. But I will have Enrico's pride in return for this favour I will do for you—understand me?'

Enrico held the phone to Freya's ear again and gave yet another nod of his head. 'Y-yes,' she repeated unsteadily.

'And will you do it?'

'Y-yes,' she whispered, wishing she knew what it was she was agreeing to.

Enrico cut the connection. He did it so abruptly that Freya blinked. Then they just stood there looking at each other, while the sound of the plastic wheels on their son's truck scraped through the stillness of the late-afternoon air.

Freya spoke first. 'What does he want?' she questioned.

'My head on a pole,' Enrico said drily, then his mouth shifted into a kind of grimace. 'You have just agreed to jilt me at the altar,' he informed her.

'Oh!' Disconcerted, she did not know what else to say without losing her cool façade.

Enrico's mouth shifted into a different expression. 'How did Luca get hold of your mobile-phone number?' he asked.

Freya instantly stiffened. The question pierced that sensitive spot called suspicion—Enrico's persistent suspicion of her.

Did he think that she'd given her number to Luca?

She pulled in a deep breath, thought about telling a lie just for the hell of paying him back…but this was just too serious to lie about.

'He stole Cindy's mobile,' she answered, then reached out to take her phone back and tilted up her chin to him. 'Would you like to play snoop again while I call Cindy up to confirm that?'

His lips flat, he nodded.

Cold-eyed and tight-throated, Freya flipped through the phone's directory until she found Cindy's land-line number and hit dial. The sound of Nicky's truck was coming closer. Any second now he was going to glance up and see his mother standing here.

'Someone pinched my mobile phone while we were out!' Cindy burst out indignantly before Freya could utter more than a husky, *Hi, it's me.* 'It had to be that red-haired bitch who sat next to me on the bus when I was on my way home,' she ranted.

Ah, that other red-haired bitch who gets mistaken for me, Freya thought coldly.

'She knocked all my bags off my lap when she sat down,' Cindy was saying. 'I thought she was being *nice* when she helped me pick up my stuff!'

'Do me a favour, Cindy, and repeat all of that to Enrico. I'm just going to hand you over to him.'

With that Freya gave Enrico the handset again, then stepped round him to go and greet her son.

Enrico let her go without saying anything.

Cindy was soon explaining how her phone had been stolen. As Enrico listened, he reacted to her mention of the red-haired woman in exactly the same way that Freya had done. He was also aware of a deep-gut relief in accepting that Cindy was not guilty of helping Luca gain access to Freya.

Freya walked past him then, with their son straddling her hips as she carried him inside. They were laughing and chatting. No one would know from her voice and her smiling expression that she'd just been put through the emotional wringer—twice.

Just as no one would know by looking at him that he felt about as distanced from the laughing chatter as a man could feel when he was still coming to terms with the fact that he had made some big, maybe irreparable, mistakes.

Then—no, he would not think like that. The damage one short hour had wrought had to be and would be reversed.

'Make sure you report the phone stolen to your provider,' he instructed Cindy. 'Freya has been receiving…nuisance calls. I will have a new phone sent around to your flat within the next hour.'

Pocketing Freya's phone, he strode into the house. It was time to get tough again, time to do what he did

best and be the ruthless troubleshooter who would take
no prisoners in his quest to make Freya Jenson his wife.

His wife! Enrico noticed the change in emphasis
from *his son* to *his wife* and actually managed a thin-
lipped smile. Maybe it had always been like that, buried
deep behind his blindness.

CHAPTER NINE

H<small>IS</small> expression set, Enrico followed the sound of his son's chatter to the kitchen and found him with Sonny, helping to feed fresh pasta through the pasta machine—but no Freya.

The two chefs looked up and smiled at him. He sent a reasonably relaxed smile back by return, then lost it the moment he'd turned out of the kitchen to head for the stairs.

He found Freya in the bedroom, sitting with her back to him on the edge of the bed, surrounded by her day's purchases as if the carnage during the hour in between had not happened.

Only this time, when Enrico got nearer, he realised her face was hidden in her hands.

His chest muscles tightened, recognising exactly the feeling behind the need to sit like that. Then he fixed his shoulders and strode further into the room, swinging the door shut behind him with enough force to make her hands drop away from her face.

She jumped to her feet, going from hopeless-looking to fierce in a second. 'I thought I told you—'

He grabbed her and kissed her. Shock tactics were the only way to go with her right now. So his lips crushed hers to stop her from yelling at him, and his hands clasped her arms to stop her from hitting out. He could feel the need vibrating from every tensed nerve ending she possessed. But she still could not stop herself from kissing him back the way she always kissed him—hungrily, greedily, helplessly.

It was his only weapon—she could not stop herself from responding to him. By the time he'd allowed their mouths to separate, his own body was aching for more. And he thought about it. Enrico stood there in front of this angry-eyed, beautiful creature and seriously considered giving in to the temptation that was rattling around inside him and just tossing them both down onto the bed and wiping out the last hour doing what they did best!

But an image of the way Luca had done that to her three years ago put such a temptation to death and he released her.

'You—you—'

'Quit the incoherent rant, *cara*,' he interrupted, moving away from her. 'I don't have time for yet another round of fighting.'

He stopped in front of the tallboy with a bunch of keys in his hand which he used to unlock the top drawer and touched a switch inside. Above the tallboy, the framed portrait of a Georgian lady hanging on the wall sprang out to reveal a safe.

Freya released a gasp because she hadn't known there was a safe hidden there! She watched Enrico remove a thick wad of paper money and a business folder, and something very close to alarm went chasing down her spine.

'W-what are you doing?' she asked warily.

He didn't answer. He just flipped the safe door shut again with long fingers and relocked the drawer.

Unable to stop herself, she took a couple of steps towards him. 'If—if that money is to pay off Luca then you're wasting it,' she advised him.

'You prefer to jilt me at the altar?'

'I prefer not to marry you at all!'

'Tough.' The money went into his pocket.

'But—don't you see?' she insisted. 'Whatever you do or whatever you say he can always make the same threats again! If you pay him for his silence, he will know he's won himself a meal ticket for life! Listen to reason.' She took another step towards him. 'It's *bad* what he can tell the Press. He doesn't *care* if it hurts Nicky. He doesn't care if most of what he says is lies! M-mud sticks, Enrico, and he wants—'

'My head on a pole,' Enrico finished for her with a nod of that dark head. 'But you confuse me. When did I say that the money is for Luca?'

Freya glanced at the folder he held in his hand. 'Th-that has his name written on it.'

Enrico looked down at the folder. 'So it does,' he agreed—then dared to look back at her and grin! 'You know, *cara*, I had forgotten what fantastic eyesight you have. Maybe it's the gorgeous green colour,' he suggested, suddenly all agitating good humour. 'I recall now how you used to read full-page documents upside down where they lay on someone's desk and shock everyone with your knowledge. It was a great resource to have on my side when you worked with me. I missed it when it was gone.'

'N-not so I noticed.'

'Look at them,' he said as he began walking towards her. 'Green as emeralds and as sharp as diamonds…'

Freya started backing away.

'Warm and sexily challenging,' he continued. 'So excitingly come-and-get-me, yet so defiantly touch-me-not cool…'

'Y-you're just changing the subject.' The end of the bed suddenly made contact with the backs of her knees.

Enrico arrived a short breath away, his eyes glinting at her, and her insides decided to enjoy the squirt of excitement that had shot down her limbs.

She put a hand out to stop him from coming closer, then had to heave in a thick breath to calm her crazily beating heart.

Sex; it was *always* sex with him!

Why? she asked herself. Why did it have to happen only with him? He wasn't her type—not really. He was too rich, too good-looking and way too charismatic for a poor and ordinary little nobody like her!

'Look…' she tried for a common sense tone '…if you will just listen to me you will see that this marriage thing is—'

'Marriage,' he interrupted, 'was the deal that we made. Marriage is the agreement we have *slept* with for two weeks.'

'But it's—'

'Our son expects it. All of Hannard's and half of Europe expect it. Are you going to turn away from me and give Luca my head on a pole?'

'It's either your head or a scandal,' she mumbled shakily.

'Then we will ride the scandal—'

'But if *you* believe what he can put out there—what chance have we got of riding out anything?'

That turned off the sexual gleam, Freya noted cynically. It did not take much to turn the seducer into a block of stone.

'You could try trusting me to resolve this.'

Freya stared aghast at him. 'What is there to trust?' she choked out. 'You are blackmailing me into marrying you and *he* is blackmailing me not to do it!'

'Then you have a dilemma,' he said unsympathetically. 'I will await your decision at the altar in two days.'

With that he turned his back on her and just walked out! Leaving Freya with the weight of his challenge hanging there.

Within the hour the whole house had been ringed by a circle of security, which did not make her feel safe at all—in fact, it did the opposite. What was it that Enrico was expecting Luca to do that he felt they needed this level of protection?

Or was the ring of security there to keep her in?

Next thing to arrive was the new mobile telephone. Bang up-to-date, state-of-the-art, iced-green in colour and sexily designed, it had all the phone numbers from her old phone saved in it—including the number of Cindy's new phone. It was only as she held it in her hand that Freya realised that Enrico had not handed her old one back to her.

For the first time in two and a half weeks she slept alone that night.

Or rather she didn't sleep, but rolled around the huge empty bed, wanting him when she should not be wanting him and despising herself for feeling that way.

Twice she reached out for the mobile phone with an impulsive need to call him and twice she stopped herself short of the deed and tossed the handset aside with a sigh.

Where was he? What was he doing? Had he had his confrontation with his cousin? Had the thick wad of money and what she'd learned was the folder of unpaid debts been enough to silence Luca's tongue? How much did the tabloids pay these days for a kiss-and-tell exposé?

Did it matter? She was sure that money was not all that Luca wanted—in fact, she knew he was quite capable of taking anything Enrico put on the table and *still* hitting them with his exposé.

Enrico did not sleep, either. He was pacing the floor in the apartment above.

He wanted her. It was a hard, nagging ache he could not stop. He needed the reassurance that he could still make her melt even while she was hating him.

Should he go down there?

He threw himself on his bed, closed his eyes and imagined her lying downstairs, curled on her side with her wonderful hair spread out behind her.

Was she wearing one of those skimpy silk night-dresses he so loved to relieve her of? What colour was it? She'd purchased a whole range of them: black, white, cream, red, the most sexy ocean-green colour that did amazing things for her eyes…

Freya got up and started pacing. Anxious, restless—agitated. He could have called her. Would it have hurt him to ring and tell her what had happened with Luca? Did he think she deserved to be kept in the dark like this?

Her phone gave a beep. She dived on it greedily. It was a text message from Enrico. 'Missing me?' it said.

She typed in an adamant, 'No,' and winged it back to him, then wished she'd ignored him because now he knew that she was awake.

Lying there naked other than for the towel he had slung round his hips, Enrico smiled as the message arrived in his inbox. She might think that she hated him, but she was awake and therefore missing him.

The tension eased from his system as he texted a second question.

'Liar,' it said. 'What colour nightdress?'

Frowning, she looked down at her skimpy ocean-green nightdress and caught an instant image of Enrico's expression of pleasure as if he were right here in this bedroom and taking her with hungry intent.

Her breasts responded, filling and tightening, making her draw in a sharp, angry breath. She hated him, she *did*. And she was never going to forgive him for what he'd done and said.

Going to sit crossed-legged on the bed, she pushed her streaming hair back from her face then set her fingers tapping.

'None of your business any more,' Enrico read. Grimacing, he sat up, drew his knees up, spreading them so he could rest his arms on them while he scanned the rest of what her message said.

'What happened with Luca?'

Now, there was a good question. 'Try trusting me, *cara*,' he sent back.

'What's to trust?' she responded; he could even hear her tartness. 'Do I jilt you at the altar or don't I?'

The cutting witch, Enrico thought ruefully. 'Your decision,' he replied.

Freya threw herself back against the pillows. She knew what he was doing. He was *demanding* she trust him. But how was she supposed to do that?

'I hate you. That's a decision,' she flung back at him, then switched her phone off and tossed it away.

'And I am falling apart loving you,' Enrico typed, then sighed and did not send it.

Declarations of that nature were best kept to himself.

He threw himself back against the pillows.

Freya curled up on her side. She wanted to weep. She had never felt so alone in her entire life. It was OK for Enrico—he had a large family in Italy ready to listen and support him if he ever needed anyone. But she had no one. Even Cindy could only be loosely called a friend. In the end, Enrico paid Cindy's wage, therefore she owed him her loyalty more than she did Freya.

Freya knew she was not going to jilt Enrico at the altar. She knew that giving in to Luca's blackmail would be about as effective at silencing him as Enrico's attempt to pay him off.

But it would be nice to be able to confide in someone, have a shoulder to cry on, a sympathetic ear in which to whisper her fears.

So you're going to marry a man who thinks you are capable of putting it out for any man. A man who only wants this marriage because you come as part of the package, along with his son.

So he still desires you—can't get enough of you in

his bed. But what happens when that desire wears thin? Does he start looking about him for someone new? And do you learn to put up with it because you know you're only in his life because Nicky needs you there?

And if you had a whole army of relatives and friends to in whom to confide all of that—would you?

No, of course you wouldn't. Pride wouldn't let you. Pride, and a need to maintain the illusion for Nicky's sake would keep your tongue still inside your head.

And she loved him, not hated him—of course she did. She just did not allow herself to think about it often, because what possible use was that love to her? Unless she was into flaying herself.

And it wasn't lack of family that was making her feel so lonely and weepy. It was missing him.

His silent mobile phone eventually got to him and Enrico climbed off the bed. Walking across the room, he flipped open the folder that contained information about Luca that had since been bulked out substantially by several revealing photographs.

His safeguard, he mused as he stared grimly at the top photograph; his secret weapon to keep Luca in check.

He could get dressed and take the photos down to show Freya. Put an end to all of the angst between them, reassure her about marrying him, then get down to some really satisfying loving in their bed.

But, juvenile of him though he knew it to be, he wanted to know if she could bring herself to trust him enough to marry him without knowing that Luca couldn't carry out his threat.

Also he owed her this in return for that early wedding present she had tossed at him.

On that dry reminder, he closed the folder and turned his back on it to go and mix himself a stiff drink.

It was going to be a long night, he considered ruefully as he threw himself onto a chair instead of the bed.

CHAPTER TEN

THEY turned out to be the longest two nights of her life.

On her wedding day, Freya tried her best to raise some enthusiasm to match that of everyone else. Nicky was over-excited, Lissa's eyes were shining because she'd managed to get a peek at the dress when it was delivered earlier that morning. Sonny was playing it cool, but even a stressed-out Freya couldn't stop her grin when he appeared looking all suave and polished in a dark three-piece suit complete with an ice-blue silk tie instead of his usual jeans and T-shirt.

No sign of Fredo today. But then Fredo would be where he usually was, shadowing his lord and master—wherever Enrico was.

Cindy had arrived while Freya was trying to bathe away the aches and creases of her second sleepless night in a row. Then suddenly the morning had gone.

Too fast. Much too fast.

In half an hour she was due at the church.

Cindy sighed as she stood back to view Freya's full effect in the mirror. 'Gosh, you look amazing,' she breathed.

Cindy's blue eyes were wearing a dewy look. But then Cindy was a fully paid-up member of the romantic dreamers' club.

Maybe this would be a good point for her to start pretending that she was, too, Freya mused as she looked at her reflection and saw the perfect romantic bride prepared for the perfect romantic wedding.

Tradition was really on a roll here. She even wore a fragile gold necklace complete with two diamond set-joined hearts that nestled lovingly in the hollow between her breasts. It had been delivered that morning with a note from Enrico.

'Be there,' was all he'd written. That was all, no reassuring words about Luca, just *be there*, like a command and a threat.

Her stomach muscles knotted.

'You're so lucky,' Cindy said softly. 'You get to marry the man of your dreams and he's such a romantic hunk.'

'You mean the asset-stripping shark with the very sharp teeth?'

Cindy laughed. 'You adore him really, so don't use that cynical tone around me. Don't you feel just a tiny bit as if none of this is real?'

All the time, Freya thought heavily. 'Any minute now my fairy godmother is going to turn up, complete with a pumpkin coach and six prancing white horses,' she mocked drily.

What they actually got was Sonny, a chauffeur and a black Bentley Continental.

The paparazzi were out in force to capture their pictures. Sonny and the chauffeur held the pack back while Freya and Cindy got into the car.

The church was one of those tiny old chapels squashed in between modern constructions, which made London the unique, crazily charming place that it was.

Five steps led up to the entrance. Lissa stood waiting inside the small foyer with a restless Nicky dressed in proper trousers, a shirt and an ice-blue silk tie like Sonny's. He looked so grown-up and cute with his dark curls combed into order that Freya's eyes tried to fill with silly tears.

Then the music started and she lost touch with ev-erything: the tears, the small clutch of people standing around her. Her heart began pounding, a bow of panic playing a rusty screech across her nerves.

This was it: the moment to make her mind up. She could run in the other direction without needing to set eyes on Enrico. She could just pick up her son and—

'OK, sweetie?' a quiet voice questioned.

She looked up at Sonny, who was looking solemnly down at her and at the same time blocking the door.

He knew. He knew what she was thinking and maybe even what she was feeling. Sonny and Fredo probably knew everything.

She moistened her lips, tasted clear gloss on the tip of her tongue. 'I can't—'

'*Si*, you can,' Sonny said firmly. Then he lowered his head to whisper, 'Trust him, *cara*.'

It always came back to that word, didn't it?

Then, as if someone had planned it, she felt a little hand slide into her hand. 'C'mon, Mummy,' Nicky said impatiently. 'We've got to go and marry Daddy.'

Marry Daddy, she repeated to herself. Did the small

boy even understand what that meant? Did he care? She was his mummy and Enrico was his daddy, just as Fredo and Sonny and Lissa were his very best friends.

The marriage had already happened, in a sense: her son was wed to these people. She needed to stop being an idiot and get in there and make it official—for him.

She let Nicky pull her across the tiny foyer. She allowed Cindy to fuss with her dress. Her heart was still pounding. Her fear of what Luca could do to them still made her feel cold with dread.

Clutching her son's hand, she took that first, tremulous step then another. She saw Enrico come to his feet at the top of the aisle. He was wearing a dark suit and his shoulders looked as if someone had strapped them to an iron bar.

There was a stir and it was then that she became aware of the congregation. She hadn't taken part in any of the arrangements. She'd just allowed herself to be carried along on the marriage wagon, buying things when she'd been told to buy them and kind of drifting through the weeks without bothering to think about this part at all.

But she had expected the chapel to be empty other than for their small wedding party, so it came as a shock to see that it was full of guests. The narrow pews were lined with row upon row of Ranieris, uncles, aunts, cousins, people who were complete strangers to her, but all with those distinctive genes that made them all look so familiar. Some were turning to stare at her curiously, others were smiling, and a few looked just plain arrogant—like the tense man who stood at the top of the aisle with his ramrod-straight back to her.

On the other side of the chapel the pews were filled with a sea of familiar faces: Hannard employees, a few wearing starry-eyed romantic smiles like Cindy's.

Enrico had done this? He'd brought all of these people together to witness their marriage without telling her? And he'd done it knowing there was a big chance she might jilt him in front of them all?

Or maybe he'd done it to add more pressure. As in— jilt me in front of this lot, if you dare.

Enrico turned then to look at her and she faltered to a complete standstill. Her heart seemed to split wide open then just fall apart. He looked exactly like what he was: a sensationally attractive, tall, dark, Italian male, wearing a fantastically cut three-piece suit and the requisite ice-blue tie.

His face was paler than it should be, which made his eyes too dark to be real. And stern—his frown was stern. His mouth looked flat, his chin taut as he stood there looking at her.

Enrico was caught, captivated. Freya's dress was exquisite: a romantic creation of fine antique lace over sensual silk. With her hair left loose and a coronet of tiny pearls holding her lace veil in place, she looked staggeringly lovely and heart-shatteringly ethereal.

She was an earth mother and fragile bride in one sensational package, with their son as her escort standing proudly at her side and her bridesmaid behind her.

But her face was so white and her eyes so dark she looked as though she were attending a wake.

Was she going to do it and jilt him? Was this why she looked so ethereal and tragic?

He felt as if he was being torn apart, his emotions spitting and crackling like a million electrodes gone wild. The music was playing and she wasn't moving. His younger brother shifted tensely at his side. Valentino did not know Freya. He'd been away in America attending university for three years. But he heard him murmur, '*Santo cielo*. Is she for real, Rico?'

Not so you could tell, Enrico thought tensely.

Then, 'Daddy!' Nicolo suddenly shouted out and a ripple of laughter ran around the chapel as the giver of the bride broke ranks to run to his father's side.

His son's hand slipped into his hand. His long fingers closed around small ones, but Enrico's eyes did not leave his bride.

Would she do it? Would she strip him of his pride in front of all of these people?

Por Dio! Come down here and finish it one way or the other. But don't just stand there looking at me as if I've died! Enrico winged his thoughts to his bride via sheer telepathy.

Freya felt as if she were standing on water, the stone floor beneath her seemed so insubstantial and unsafe. It was seeing her son and her lover standing there looking at her, both dark-haired and dark-eyed, that made it feel that frail.

As if she could hear what she was thinking, Cindy stepped up to Freya. 'They belong to you. Go and get them,' she whispered.

Freya's feet began to move again. She saw a nerve flick along Enrico's tense jaw. The music was still playing, people were whispering. As she came closer Fredo stepped up from seemingly nowhere and bent to lift Nicky into his big arms.

Then it was just the two of them with the priest, and they had the ceremony to get through. Each time Freya was expected to speak, Enrico felt his heartbeat go crazy, each soft and tremulous response she gave hitting his libido hard.

She did it, though; she got through the ceremony with only one heart-stopping moment when the priest asked if there was any reason why the marriage should not take place, and in the throat-cutting silence that followed her cold fingers shook in Enrico's hands.

They did all the legal stuff without speaking to each other. Valentino introduced himself to Freya, then welcomed her into the family with truck-loads of Ranieri charm. Jealousy ripped through Enrico, a greedy, dark, possessive jealousy, because she smiled for Valentino but she had stopped looking at him at all.

He watched her eyes hunt the mass of Ranieri faces as she and he walked back along the aisle. He could feel her tension, her fear that Luca was going to jump out at any minute and slur their names in front of everyone.

He must have been mad to put her to the test like this, Enrico thought on a sudden burst of anger. Who the hell did he think he was, playing with her feelings like this?

The Press were there in force to capture their reports and pictures. No one could say they did not make the perfect image of romance as they stood on the church steps with their son standing between them with one of his big grins on his face.

Cindy stood just behind them chatting to Valentino. Everyone looked relaxed, except for Freya.

The sooner he got them away from here the better, Enrico decided as the fixed smile he was wearing began to make his jaw ache.

He scanned the wedding party, looking for Fredo to give him the nod to come and collect Nicolo, but a flash of red from across the street suddenly caught his eye.

The bastard, he thought as he recognised the hair colour. Luca just could not resist it. Despite everything they'd agreed, Luca could not let this moment pass without trying to cause trouble.

Bending down, Enrico scooped Nicolo onto his arm then clamped the other round Freya's waist and hurried them down the steps and hustled them into the waiting car.

With a curt command the car shot off from the kerb before Enrico had even secured Nicolo as best as he could, as his son's safety seat wasn't installed. He waited for Freya to say something about that but she didn't. In fact, they did not speak at all on the short journey to the country club he'd commandeered to house his family for the weekend. Nicky did all the talking. They answered him in turn.

The moment they stepped into the country-club foyer Enrico said tautly, 'Freya…'

'I saw her,' she responded and walked off, following signs that showed the way to the ladies' room.

Nicolo ran off then. By the time Enrico had gone after him and prevented the toddler from causing mayhem, their guests were arriving, so all he could do was to stand there and crack stupid jokes about his missing bride.

Pale but composed, Freya reappeared beside him. Enrico grabbed and grimly held on to her hand.

Freya got through the welcoming ceremony. She even got through the wedding breakfast without falling apart. But her eyes could not stop hunting for a glimpse of the redhead, or worse—the darker head of Luca himself.

Then it happened. Everyone was circulating nicely. She'd seen that Cindy was with a group of work colleagues, Fredo and Sonny were talking to a group of Ranieris. Enrico was standing a couple of feet away from her, listening intently to something one of his uncles was saying to him, and she noticed Lissa blushingly flirting with a Ranieri nephew or cousin by the open French windows that led out into the club's grounds.

But no Nicky.

Her heart froze for a moment as an alarm bell went off inside her head. It was her chilling sixth sense that took her towards her son's nanny. It took only a distracted glance beyond the French windows to send her blood running colder still.

Enrico turned to look for Freya just as it happened— one small step, then another, and she was off and running, crashing past Lissa and out through the open doors.

A curse left his throat as he took off after her. There was only one thing that would send her running like that and it was their son!

Freya hit the terrace like a sprinter, losing her shoes on the way down the steps that led onto a wide spread of lawn, which connected the country club to a golf course.

Out there in front of her, she could see Luca squatting down at Nicky's level. The little boy was reaching out to take back the small football Lissa had brought along with them to stop him from becoming bored.

Freya's veil went next, finest lace tearing from her hair and floating away on the wind.

Enrico saw her discarded shoes as he leapt down the steps. Something like a light bulb lit up inside his head then shattered into hot fragments when he caught sight of what had made her run.

'The crazy idiot,' he muttered. 'Freya—stop, for *Dio's* sake!'

But Freya was stopping for no one. All she could see was that Luca was going to get his own back by kidnapping her son! The man looked round for a short second before she reached him and she caught a blurred glimpse of his dark eyes widening just before she threw herself on him, knocking him off balance so the two of them went sprawling on the ground.

Nicky started laughing. He thought it was hilarious. Enrico ripped out another thick curse as he bent down to pluck up his wife.

His crazy wife!

'Stop it,' he hissed out when she began fighting him as well. Then, more gently, he cajoled, '*Cara*, this is Valentino. You just tackled *Valentino*…'

Freya stopped fighting Enrico to look at him through bright, fear-blinded eyes. Her breathing was haywire, her green eyes wild. Enrico wanted to kiss her. He wanted to do it so badly he almost gave in to the urge.

Nothing was making sense to Freya any longer. She felt as if she'd been turned inside out and upside down.

Nicky was still laughing and now he had jumped on top of his new uncle. Valentino was letting him do it while he just lay there staring up at her.

Reality began to sink in. 'Y-you aren't Luca,' she heard herself whisper.

'*Dio*. I hope not,' said Valentino. 'Did you think that I was?'

'He—he…'

'She is very protective of our son, Tino,' Enrico put in gruffly. 'It would have been better if you had let someone know you were bringing him out here to play football.'

'But I did,' said the younger man. 'I told his nanny.'

Valentino rose to his feet with the same grace as his older brother possessed—in fact, he was the same height as Enrico, Freya noticed hazily. The same strength in his features, the same—

'I'm s-sorry,' she whispered.

'No need.' The younger man grinned. He even used the same easy care as Enrico would to balance Nicky on his arm. 'I quite enjoyed being bowled over by my brother's bride.'

His brother wasn't so pleased about it. He had Freya clamped against him like a vice.

With a grim nod of his head, Enrico instructed Valentino to make himself scarce.

'More football,' Nicky demanded as Valentino carried him away from the bride and groom.

'Sure, little one,' his uncle said agreeably. 'But first we will find a place where your mamma will not see us and want to join in.'

Freya laughed, but it was a very short laugh and actually closer to a sob.

Enrico didn't laugh. He was frowning at the mass of curious people standing out on the terrace trying to understand what was going on.

'Shall we go the whole way and I will put you across my knee and beat you?' he murmured unpleasantly. 'That way they will believe that we are both insane.'

'Y-you don't understand w-what...'

Air hissed from him angrily. Lightning flashes sparked from his eyes because he did understand, and he also knew whose fault it was that the incident had happened.

'He looked like Luca—'

'I will insult him with that observation later.'

'I j-just saw him with Nicky, and after seeing the redhead at the church I...'

'I have changed my mind about your excellent eyesight,' Enrico interrupted. 'You are really quiet stunningly blind!'

'There's no need to be nasty because I made a mistake!' she choked out.

'Your mistake, *cara*, is believing that the redhead and Luca are two different people!' he raked out.

Freya's chin shot up. Their eyes clashed. It was the first time it had happened since she arrived at the church. Enrico's insides flipped over then took one of those steep, sinking dives.

'What did you say?' she breathed up at him.

'Nothing,' he denied tensely.

'But y-you said—'

'We are not going to do this here!' he raked out.

'We will do it right here!' Freya insisted.

'What—fight? Shout at each other? Give everyone up there something to really talk about, when I decide to go to hell with the whole damn thing and roll you back down on the ground for myself?'

Freya took a step back, hair flying away from her face in the light warmth of the summer breeze, arms tense at her sides crushing the fragile antique lace of her gown.

'Explain what you just said,' she insisted stubbornly.

'Green-eyed little witch,' he muttered, grabbed her by the waist, lifted her off the ground and kissed her—hard.

He needed it. He'd needed to do this for too many damn frustrating days to make the kiss anything but hungry. What he did not expect was for her slender arms to curve around his neck and that she would kiss him back with the same ravenous need.

Yet he should have expected it. Didn't she always respond like this for him?

He pulled his lips away. 'We are getting away from here,' he gritted.

Green pools of gorgeous, sensuous helplessness drowned him. 'OK,' was all she said.

Just like that—*just* like that!

Madre de Dio, if he did not hang on to some control here he was going to carry out his threat and roll her back down on the grass!

He placed her back on her own two feet again. Shoeless feet. He flexed his shoulders as a rush of arousal swept in. 'Pretty damn kinky,' he muttered to himself. Then he was grabbing her hand and turning to stride across the grass, hauling his bride behind him.

The closer Freya got to the terrace full of guests the less she wanted to see them. When Enrico bent to pick up her veil from the grass, she wished he would toss it over her burning face. At the steps he stopped to gather up her shoes. By then a kind of sizzling fascination was holding their audience rapt.

Enrico ignored them, every single last one of them—uncles, aunts, employees. Arrogantly he let them part like the waves to allow him access into the country club and Freya kept her head down so she didn't make eye contact with anyone.

He didn't stop walking until they had left the club by the front entrance. Rows of limos lined the car park. Enrico headed for the Bentley, dismissed the driver and propelled Freya inside. Her shoes were laid on the floor beside her feet. The gossamer-fine drift of her lace veil arrived on her lap. Enrico eased himself into the driver's seat, looking so gorgeous and obviously pulsing with testosterone that Freya was held silent and breathless as he started the engine then drove them away from their wedding reception.

Had their guests followed them to witness their departure like this? She didn't know, did not look back to find out. Sex was in the driving seat when she knew she should not let it be. It filled every nook and cranny inside the luxurious car and inside herself.

'Where are we going?' she dared to ask him.

'Home,' he said.

Home as in London or Milan?

It was then that she remembered something she should not have forgotten. 'But what about Nicky? We—'

Tight-lipped, he reached out and flicked on the radio. Heavy rock music suddenly blasted her out.

She knew what he was doing. He was blocking out

the reminder because their son did not have a place in what was happening right now.

But Freya was beginning to regroup her senses. She was also replaying what he'd said at the country club. Did he really think that she was going to lie down on a bed somewhere and let him make love to her, while Luca Ranieri still hovered over them like some dark, leering spectre?

Anger began to simmer, because she'd let him get away without explaining that thing he'd said about Luca, which still did not make any sense to her.

They arrived at the Mayfair house. She should have known that *home* meant the nearest place he owned with a bed. The car engine stopped, so did the rock music.

Instantly she burst into agitated speech. 'Don't think I'm going to let you just walk me in there and…'

Enrico got out of the car and shut the door.

Beginning to feel just a bit fevered now, Freya stuffed her feet into her shoes. He already had her door open and was waiting for her to get out of the car. Clutching her veil, she climbed out onto the pavement and stalked right past him, then had to wait while he used his key to open the front door.

She was about to step inside when he scooped her up into his arms.

'W-what do you—?'

'Tradition,' he gritted, as he strode across the threshold then shouldered the door shut behind him.

'The tradition thing wore thin ages ago,' she derided. 'So you can put me down.'

'When I now understand why I must carry you?' he

quizzed grimly. 'This way I maintain the upper hand until I have you exactly where I want you.'

Since he was already climbing the stairs, Freya did not need to ask where. He kicked the bedroom door shut behind them and strode towards the bed.

None of this should be happening—none of it! she told herself as the feverish sensation grew worse.

'No,' she protested, only to feel the hard cut of disappointment when he let her feet slip to the floor then took a step back.

His dark head went back. 'What, then?' he challenged arrogantly.

'Explain that—thing you said about Luca,' she insisted.

She had eyes he wanted to drown in and a body beneath the virginal dress that was seething with wanton lust. Did she think she was fooling him with the stubbornness? Did she think he could not tell that she wanted what he wanted as badly as he did?

His hand went into his inside jacket pocket and withdrew an envelope—a gold envelope. He handed it to her then turned and walked across the room to the tallboy.

'What is it?'

'Look,' he suggested, using the key to unlock the wall safe.

The Georgian lady sprang away from the wall while Enrico listened to Freya breaking the envelope seal. His fingers were not steady as he reached inside the open safe.

She'd gone very quiet now. He turned to look at her. As usual her hair was tumbling around her lowered face.

'We see what we expect to see,' he fed across the room to her. 'What do you see, *cara*?'

She gave a small shake of her head. 'I can't believe it,' she whispered.

'I cannot say that I readily believed it when I walked into his hotel suite and saw it for myself.'

Freya looked up. Enrico was leaning against the tallboy, all sartorial elegance and sophisticated grace. Her senses leapt. She crushed them down again.

'You just—walked in?'

'Luca has always liked to do things the easy way. And using the Ranieri name to gain him the good things in life, including the best in accommodation, has always been expensive—for me. He might have been thrown out of the family, but I have been picking up the tab for his high-life ever since. The hotel he was staying in belongs to me,' he explained. 'So access to his suite was relatively easy.'

'And…' He watched intently as she moistened her lips. 'And you caught him—like this?'

'Exactly like that. Quite revealing, hmm?'

Freya looked back at the photograph she held in her fingers, which showed Luca close up and full in the face. He was sporting a red-haired wig and a beautifully cut slinky black dress. His make-up was simply perfect. He looked—disconcertingly beautiful.

'I had the foresight to use my phone to take pictures while he was recovering from the shock.' Enrico had many more of them stashed in Luca's folder, but the one Freya was holding said it all.

'He is not gay, in case you are wondering. He simply likes to dress up in women's clothes. His latest mistress finds it…exciting. But she is not excited about his running costs. So when we appeared in the newspapers he believed he had found himself a new income—just as you had predicted he would.'

'Blackmail.'

'With a sense of humour.' Enrico nodded. 'Hence the staged appearances as the redhead. He always was a twisted son of a bitch.'

'Did you already know a-about this?'

Enrico shook his head. 'None of the family knows, which meant I had stumbled upon the best weapon I had to shoot down his blackmailing plans. He would rather run back down his dark hole and never emerge again than have the Ranieris know his little secret.'

'But he turned up at the church today in front of the whole Ranieri family!'

Enrico grimaced. 'I have to confess that I don't know why he did that unless…' He pushed out a sigh then straightened up to turn back to the safe. 'He hates me, *cara*,' he said. 'For being born to inherit the Ranieri power instead of him. I used to turn a blind eye to his envy because, in a way, I understood it and I actually *cared* about him, but…'

The words stopped but the expression on his face said the rest for him. 'There's nothing wrong with loving someone who does not love you back,' Freya said huskily.

His shoulders flexed. 'It makes you a weaker person.'

'Yes,' she agreed.

'Vulnerable,' he added.

Freya pulled in her bottom lip to stop herself from answering that, unsure where he was going to take it.

'You are forever striving to make them see you in a better light.'

'You paid his debts off.'

'Yes.'

'You gave him the money.'

'Though I had no need to,' he agreed. 'Yet Luca could not resist turning up today for one last thrust of the knife. He wanted me to know that if he wanted to he could "come out" and my hold on him would be gone.'

But there was more to this than just Luca playing devil's advocate. 'You still believe his version about what happened three years ago,' she whispered as her heart spun into a painful twist.

'Are you crazy?' he turned round to look at her at last. 'Of course I don't!'

'Then why the big tear-jerking confession about the vulnerability of loving someone?' she threw back.

'Here—catch.' He tossed something at her.

Freya had to drop the photograph to field what had arrived in her hands. It was a DVD case. She frowned at it.

'Your wedding present,' he explained—and she did not miss the point being made in the way it had been delivered. 'I am a man who likes to cover all contingencies, *cara*. Getting Luca to give me a full and honest confession about what happened three years ago was a safeguard I recorded via my mobile then downloaded to DVD. I did think of going for the big matching gesture and having a printed version mounted and framed for you but I was afraid you might hang it in the hall where everyone could read it and see what a blind and vulnerable idiot I am.'

'Vulnerable how?' Her head came up.

He sent her one of those lazy, rueful smiles because she was not questioning the blind-idiot part.

'Frightened,' he expanded. 'That here came another person I—cared about, who held me in contempt for feeling that way.'

'You *wanted* to believe his version!' Freya accused him.

'I was as weak as a kitten,' he continued. 'Besotted; with your hair, your eyes and—'

'You stay back there until we have finished this!' she warned when he began to move.

'—And scared because the marriage thing was hitting panic buttons inside my head even before I saw you with him.'

'So you *preferred* to believe I could betray you because that let you off the commitment hook?'

He caught her, crushing sensual silk and lace to lift her right off the ground and bring their eyes level. Hers were sparking, his were just black…

Sexy black, contrite black…an I-know-where-I-am-going-with-this kind of arrogantly challenging black.

'I love you like there is no tomorrow,' he told her softly.

'Well, that makes it all OK then, doesn't it?' Freya flashed back sarcastically even as the declaration sent her heart into a dizzy, dipping dive.

'Why can't you cut me a bit of slack?' Enrico sighed out.

'Because you're aroused,' she said in disgust.

'You think you need to tell me that?'

'And you're crazy if you think I am going to—'

'I married you because I am crazy,' he put in as he

turned with her still clamped to his body. 'Mad,' he expanded. 'Cut up. Gut-wrenchingly guilty. On fire. In love. Scared of it and you and of losing it all again because I had been too blind to see the truth three years ago.'

'Because *he* told you the truth at last?'

'Because *you* told me the truth,' he sighed out impatiently. 'Because *you* made me open my eyes and *see* that damn truth!'

She opened her mouth to say something. He kissed her to stop her from arguing and she fell into the kiss the way she always did.

None of this should be happening—none of it! Freya told herself as the familiar fever erupted and she could not stop herself from responding. They still had things to discuss!

'Later…' he murmured.

He could even read her mind now. 'OK,' she heard herself mumble weakly—and recaptured his mouth.

Just like that—*just* like that!

'*Madre de Dio*, you are a contrary creature,' he gritted out as he stopped beside the bed and let her feet touch the floor so he could start taking his clothes off.

'Let me,' she said and flipped his hands away so her own could do the job.

It was like unwrapping the best wedding present ever. Her man, her possession—she had the vow of love and the gold wedding ring to prove it.

She laughed.

He growled something not very pleasant about teasing women, then sent her flying backwards onto the bed and followed her.

The dress could have been a rag. Maybe she should have married him in a rag, bearing in mind the lack of care and respect he used for the exquisite fabric of her wedding dress as he removed it.

His shirt was hanging open, his trousers half undone. While she knelt up so he could deal with the million and one tiny buttons down the back of her dress, she was busy removing his shoes and socks.

'No finesse—*no* finesse,' she accused the both of them. 'And it's my proper wedding night!'

'We will do the finesse bit later,' he assured her as the dress fell away to reveal sheer lace-cupped breasts that pouted creamily and a shapely backside dressed in almost nothing at all.

He smoothed his hands possessively over her rear. He leant forward and buried his teeth in its tight satin flesh. She quivered with pleasure and raked off his trousers.

After that, everything was forgotten as passion took over: hungry, sensory, hot, greedy, giving, taking, lusty and loving passion....

More adjectives, Freya thought hazily. Good adjectives. Beautiful, meaningful, wonderful adjectives.

'I love you so much,' she sighed out.

His hand curved around her nape, gently tugging it back so he could look into her eyes. It was there. Their greenness was lit by a love he had seen three years before, but only now did he realise that it had been missing recently.

'I don't deserve you,' he responded roughly.

'I know,' she smiled. 'Aren't you lucky? And you never know, if I'm very persistent I might even get you to say the love word again.'

His dark eyes began to gleam. 'Maybe, if you press all the right buttons.'

'Ah,' she said. It was a challenge. 'What about this button…?'

'You green-eyed witch,' he groaned. 'Yes. *Si—si—si…!*'

If you enjoyed what you just read,
then we've got an offer you can't resist!

Take 2 bestselling love stories FREE!

Plus get a FREE surprise gift!

THREE MORE FREE BOOKS!

HARLEQUIN *Presents*

This September, purchase 6 Harlequin Presents books and get these THREE books for FREE!

IN THE BANKER'S BED
by Cathy Williams

CITY CINDERELLA
by Catherine George

AT THE PLAYBOY'S PLEASURE
by Kim Lawrence

To receive the THREE FREE BOOKS above, please send us 6 (six) proofs
of purchase from Harlequin Presents books to the addresses below.

- -

Name (PLEASE PRINT)

Address   **Apt. #**

City   **State/Prov.**   **Zip/Postal Code**

098 KKL DXJP

www.eHarlequin.com